Under the heading " ⬚ *had typed a neat sch* ⬚*

    Tuesday: 7 p.m., bike to Maynard's, ice cream

    Friday: 7:30 p.m., movie at the old Tivoli

    Sunday: 3 p.m., swim at Blue Rock, weather permitting

For a man who had taken weekend trips to
Monte Carlo, who had been wined and dined in
the most famous restaurants in the world, her plan
should have been laughable. This was what she had
come up with for excitement? This was the courtship
of Miss Sophie?

But, oddly, Brand didn't feel like laughing. He felt as if
he was choking on something. The choices not made, a
sweet way of life left behind.

The second sheet, also neatly typed, was titled
"Courtship Guidelines." As he scanned it, he realized
these really were Sophie's rules, starting with no public
demonstrativeness and ending with the request that he
not call her Sweet Pea.

"Oh, lady," he said, crumpling up the rules, needing to
regain his equilibrium. "You have so much to learn."

Dear Reader,

I always use humor in my writing, because I think laughter is one of the best parts of all relationships. We've been together twenty years and my guy, Rob, still makes me laugh out loud. So I was thrilled to be asked to write a romantic comedy for Harlequin® Romance.

What I didn't expect was that I would be facing a tragedy as I wrote.

As you will see from my dedication, my friend Judy died while I was working on this story. I had the great privilege of being able to spend time with her every day for the last weeks of her life. When I delivered her eulogy I said I felt I had experienced love at its truest and deepest and most breathtaking in those final days with Judy.

I came away with a sense of having been inspired by Judy's courage, humility and grace. Her final gifts to me were these: spirit is in life *and* death, in joy *and* sorrow; it is profoundly present in every single sacred breath. Laughter is a light that can pierce the deepest dark. And finally, love is an energy so powerful it cannot be destroyed. Love truly is forever.

My greatest wish is that this book honors Judy by bringing you, the reader, moments where you experience each of those three elements.

I am yours in spirit, in laughter and in love.

Cara

CARA COLTER
Winning a Groom in 10 Dates

The Fun Factor

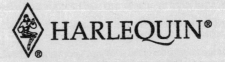
HARLEQUIN®

TORONTO • NEW YORK • LONDON
AMSTERDAM • PARIS • SYDNEY • HAMBURG
STOCKHOLM • ATHENS • TOKYO • MILAN • MADRID
PRAGUE • WARSAW • BUDAPEST • AUCKLAND

Recycling programs
for this product may
not exist in your area.

ISBN-13: 978-0-373-17672-4

WINNING A GROOM IN 10 DATES

First North American Publication 2010.

Copyright © 2010 by Cara Colter.

Cara Colter lives on an acreage in British Columbia with her partner, Rob, and eleven horses. She has three grown children and a grandson. She is a recent recipient of an *RT Book Reviews* Career Achievement Award in the Love and Laughter category. Cara loves to hear from readers; you can contact her or learn more about her through her Web site, www.cara-colter.com.

In Loving Memory
Judy Michelle Moon
1949–2009

PROLOGUE

"I SEE you've lost the hippie hair and the face stubble and the earring, Sheridan."

"Yes, sir." Brand had been so deep undercover for so long, answering to his own name was difficult.

"You don't even look like him anymore," his boss said approvingly. "Brian Lancaster is dead. We made it look as if his private plane went down over the Mediterranean under suspicious circumstances. No one in what's left of the Looey's operation will be questioning why Mr. Lancaster wasn't one of the twenty-three arrests made across seven different countries.

"Amazing work, Sheridan. None of us could have predicted this when you answered that ad on the Internet. You took FREES in a new direction."

FREES, First Response Emergency Eradication Squad, was an antiterrorism unit made up of tough, highly disciplined men with specialty training. Brand, recruited right after his first tour of active duty with the marines, had physical prowess and a fearlessness that had made him a top vertical-rescue specialist. But it was that gift, along with his knowledge of languages, that had earmarked him for FREES.

Answering an Internet ad out of Europe that offered

to buy highly restricted weapons had changed everything. Brand had found himself moving away from his specialty, immersed in a murky world where he was part cop, part soldier, part agent, part operative.

But it had taken its toll. The truth was, Brand preferred hard assignments as opposed to soft ones—assignments where training and physical strength came together in a rush of activity, in and out, and over. It didn't mess with your head as much as the past four years had. He longed for the relative simplicity of being an expert at something as technical as rope rescue.

"Look, even though it looks like Lancaster bit the dust, we've got a bit of mop-up to do. Bit players, loose ends. You need to lie low for a while. Really low. As if you really did disappear off the face of the earth. Know any place to do that?"

Brand Sheridan knew *exactly* where he could do that. The kind of place where no one would ever look for the likes of Brian Lancaster. A place of tree-lined, shady streets, where no one locked their doors, and the scent of petunias cascading out of window boxes perfumed the night air. It was a place where the big excitement on Friday night was the Little League game in Harrison Park.

It was the place that had piqued his fascination with all things that took a man high off the ground, but it had also been the place his younger self couldn't wait to get away from.

And the truth was, he dreaded going back there now. But he had to.

"I've got some leave coming, sir." That was an understatement. Brand Sheridan had been undercover for four years. The deeper in he got, the less the assignment had lent itself to taking holidays.

He'd been so good at what he did, had achieved the

results he had, because of his ability to immerse himself in that world, to play that role as if his life depended on it.

Which it had.

His boss was looking askance at him.

"I need to go home."

The word *home* felt as foreign to him as answering to his own name had done.

"It'll be safe there?"

"If you were looking for a hidey-hole, the place where someone like Brian Lancaster would be least likely to be found? Sugar Maple Grove would be it."

"One-horse town?"

"Without the horse," he said wryly. "On the edge of the Green Mountains, Vermont. As far as I know, they still have a soda fountain and the kids ride their bikes to school. The big deal is the annual yard tour and rose show."

He hesitated. "My sister has been in touch. She's afraid my dad's not coping very well with the death of my mother. I need to go see if he's okay."

Not that his father would appreciate it. At all.

"Your mother died while you were out, didn't she?"

Her pride and joy the fact her yard had been on that annual tour of spectacular gardens, that her roses had been prize-winners. "Yes, sir."

"I'm sorry. I know we weren't able to bring you in when it happened."

"That's the nature of the job, sir." And only people who did that job, like the man sitting across from him, could fully get that.

His father, the small-town doctor? Not so much.

"Good work on Operation Chop-Looey," his boss said. "Exceptional. Your name has been put in for a commendation."

Brand said nothing. He'd lived in a shadowy world

where you were rewarded for your ability to pretend, your ability to betray the people you befriended and led to trust you. Getting a commendation for that? At this point he had mixed feelings about what he had done and about himself. One of those feelings definitely wasn't pride.

He didn't really want to go back to Sugar Maple Grove. His father was angry, and rightfully so. His sister had given him an unsavory assignment.

So, at the same time Brand Sheridan dreaded going back there, he was aware something called him that he could not run from anymore...

"I should be able to wrap up what I need to do in Sugar Maple in a week, two tops." Brand asked.

"Let's give it a month. That will give us time to put some protective measures in place for you."

A month in Sugar Maple Grove? He hadn't expected to stay that long. What on earth was he going to find to do there for a month?

But Brand Sheridan didn't have the kind of job where you argued with the boss.

"Yes, sir," he said, and to himself he thought, *maybe I'll catch up on my sleep.*

CHAPTER ONE

STARS studded an inky summer sky. Bright sparks drifted upward to dance briefly with fireflies before disappearing forever. It was the perfect night to say good-bye.

"Good-bye," Sophie Holtzheim said out loud. "Good-bye foolish romantic notions and dreams."

Her voice sounded small and lonely against the stillness of the night, the voice of a woman who was saying farewell to the future she had planned out so carefully for herself.

Sophie was in her aging neighbor's backyard. She was taking advantage of the fact he was away for the night to utilize his fire pit, though the absolute privacy of his huge yard and mature landscaping had irresistible appeal, too.

Sophie's own house, in this 1930s neighborhood of Craftsman-style homes, was next to this one, on a Sugar Maple Grove corner lot. Despite a barrier of thick dogwood hedges surrounding her property, she did not want to risk a late-night dog-walker catching a glimpse of a fire burning…or of a woman in a white dress muttering to herself.

Let's face it: when a woman was wearing her wedding dress, alone, at midnight on a Saturday, she wanted guaranteed privacy. And reprieve from the small-town rumor mill.

Sophie Holtzheim had fueled that quite enough over the past six months!

Taking a deep breath, Sophie smoothed a hand over the white silk of her wedding gown. She had loved it instantly, with its simple spaghetti straps, non-dramatic V-neck, fabric floating in a subtle A-line to the ground.

"I am never going to walk down the aisle in this dress." She hoped to sound firm, resolved, *accepting*. She hoped saying it out loud would help, somehow, but it didn't.

Sighing, Sophie opened the lid of the box beside her, and contemplated its contents.

"Good-bye," she whispered.

It was a wedding-in-a-box. Inside were printer's samples of invitations and name plates, patterns for bridesmaids' dresses, magazine cuttings of flower arrangements and table settings, brochures for dream honeymoon destinations.

Sophie forced herself to pick up the invitation sample that sat on the very top of the bulging box.

"Don't read it," she ordered herself. "Just throw it in the fire."

Naturally, she did no such thing. In the flickering light of the bonfire she had roaring in Dr. Sheridan's stone-lined pit, she ran her hand over the raised cream-colored lettering of the printer's sample. It was the invitation she had selected for her wedding.

"This day," she read, "two become one. Mr. and Mrs. Harrison Hamilton invite you to join them in a celebration of love as their son, Gregg, joins his life to that of Miss Sophie Holtzheim…."

With a choking sob, Sophie tossed the invitation into

the fire, watched its ivory edges turn brown and curl before it burst into flame.

Gregg was not joining his life to Miss Sophie Holtzheim. He was joining his life to Antoinette Roberts.

For the past few months Sophie had held out hope that this was all going to get better, that Gregg would come to his senses.

But that hope had been dashed this afternoon when she had been handed a brand-new invitation, with Antoinette Roberts's name on it. *Instead of hers.*

It wasn't a wedding invitation, but an invitation to an engagement celebration at Gregg's parents' posh estate on the outskirts of Sugar Maple Grove.

"Gregg and I were engaged. We never had an engagement party." Sophie felt ridiculously slighted that all stops were being pulled out for the *new* fiancée.

It was the final straw and set the tears that had been building all afternoon flowing freely. She was glad she hadn't applied any makeup for her good-bye-hopes-and-dreams ceremony!

How could Claudia Hamilton, Gregg's mother, do this to her? Sophie was the one who was supposed to be marrying Gregg. It was too cruel to invite her to the engagement party where all of Sugar Maple Grove would be introduced to the woman Gregg had replaced Sophie with!

But his mother, who had once pored over the bridal magazines with Sophie, had made her motivations very clear.

"It can't look like we're snubbing you, dear. The whole town is going to be there. And you *must* come. For your own good. Your split was months ago. You don't want to start looking pathetic. Try not to come alone. Try to look as if you're getting on with your life."

Meaning, of course, it was way too obvious that she wasn't.

"We can't have the whole town talking *forever* about Gregg breaking the heart of the town sweetheart. It will be bad for his and Toni's new law practice. It's really not fair that he's looking like the villain in all this, is it, Sophie?"

No, it wasn't. This whole catastrophe was of Sophie's own making.

"If only I could take it back," she whispered, as she rubbed a fresh cascade of tears from her cheeks. If only she could take back the words she had spoken.

She relived them now, adding fuel to the fire in front of her in the form of a picture of a wedding cake, three tiers, yellow roses trailing down the sides.

"Gregg," she'd said, as he was heading back to South Royalton to complete law school, and pressing her to set a date for their wedding, "I need some time to think."

Now she had her whole life to *think,* to mull over the fact she had thrown everything away over a case of cold feet.

The truth was Sophie had thought she'd known Gregg as well as she knew herself. But she could never have predicted how Gregg would react. She had pictured him being gently understanding. But in actual fact, Gregg had been furious. How dare *she* need time to think about *him?* And who could blame him really?

The Hamiltons were Sugar Maple Grove royalty.

And Sophie Holtzheim was just the sweet geek whom the whole town had come to know and love for putting Sugar Maple Grove on the map a decade ago as a finalist in the National Speech Contest with, "What Makes a Small Town Tick."

Even years after she'd shed the braces and glasses, Sophie had never quite shed her geeky image.

So, naturally, she'd been bowled over when Gregg Hamilton had noticed *her*.

If he seemed a little preoccupied with how things looked to others, and if he had always been more pragmatic than romantic, those could hardly be considered flaws.

Especially in retrospect!

But it hadn't been those things that bothered her. It had been something else, something she couldn't name, just below the surface where she couldn't see it, identify it. It had niggled, and then wiggled, and then huffed, and then puffed and then, finally, it had blown her whole world apart.

Because when she couldn't ignore it for one more second, when her stomach hurt all the time, and she couldn't sleep, she had told Gregg, hesitantly, apologetically, *I can't put my finger on it. Something's wrong. Something's missing.* And she'd slid the huge solitaire diamond off her finger and given it back to him.

But nothing could have prepared Sophie for the startling swiftness of Gregg's reaction. He had replaced her. Rumors that Gregg had been dating a new girl around the campus had found their way home within weeks of her returning his ring.

Sophie had thought he was just trying to make her jealous. Surely what they'd had was not so superficial that Gregg could replace her within weeks?

But today, hand-delivered confirmation had come that, no, he wasn't trying to make her jealous. She *really* had been replaced. It was no joke. He was not on the rebound. He was not going to realize that Antoinette, beautiful and brilliant as she might be, was no replacement for Sophie. Gregg was not going to come back to her. Ever. An invitation to an engagement party could not be rationalized away.

It was final. It was over. *Over.*

Claudia had instructed her not to become pathetic. Was it too late? Was she already pathetic? Was that how everyone saw her?

If Claudia Hamilton could see Sophie now, conducting her druidlike ceremony, hunched over her box of dreams in a dress she would never wear again, it would no doubt confirm the diagnosis.

Pathetic. Burning up her box of dreams, reliving those fateful words and wondering what would have happened if she had never spoken them...

"I am not going to that party," she said, out loud, her voice strong and sure for the first time. "Never. Wild horses could not drag me there. I don't care how it *looks* to the Hamiltons."

There. She relished her moment of absolute strength and certainty for the millisecond that it lasted.

And then she crumpled.

"What have I done?" she wailed.

What had she done?

"I wanted to feel on fire," she said mournfully. "I threw it all away for that." She sat in the silence of the night contemplating her rashness.

Suddenly the hair on the back of her neck rose. She *sensed* him before she saw him. A scent on the wind? An almost electrical change in the velvety texture of the summer night?

Someone had come into the yard. She knew it. Had come in silently, and was watching her. How long had he been there? Who was it? She could feel something hotter than the fire burning the back of her neck.

She turned her head, carefully. For a moment, she saw nothing. And then she saw the outline of a man, blacker than the night shadows.

He was standing silently just inside the gate, so still he didn't even seem to be breathing. He was over six feet of pure physical presence, his stance both alert and calm, like a predatory cat, a cougar.

Sophie's heart began to hammer. But not with fear. With recognition.

Even though the darkness shrouded his features, even though it had been eight years since he had stood in this yard, even though his body had matured into its full power, Sophie *knew* exactly who he was.

The man who had wrecked her life.

And it wasn't the same man whose name was beside hers on a mock-up wedding invitation, either.

It was the one she had thought of when she'd made that fateful statement that she needed some time to think. That *something* was missing.

Oh, she hadn't named him, not even in her own mind. But she had *felt* a longing for something only he, Brand Sheridan, wayward doctor's son, wanderer of the world, had ever made her feel.

She knew it was ridiculous to toss her whole life away on something that had begun whispering to her when she was a preteen, and had become all-consuming by the time she was fifteen years old.

But there was no substitute for that feeling. It was like the swoosh in the pit of your stomach when you jumped off the cliff at Blue Rock. There was a thrilling suspended moment after the decision to go and before you hit the ice-cold pool of water, where you felt it. Intensely alive. Invigorated. As if that one glorious moment was all that mattered.

Brand had made her feel that. *Always.* She'd been twelve when her family had moved in next door to his, he'd been seventeen.

Just setting eyes on him had been enough to make her whole day go as topsy-turvy as her insides. Filled with a kind of wonder, and an impossible hope.

Sophie had loved the man who stood behind her in the darkness as desperately as only a young teen could love. She had loved him unrealistically, furiously, unrequitedly.

The fact that she had been only the teeniest glitch on Brand Sheridan's radar had intensified her feelings instead of reducing them.

She felt the familiar shiver in her belly—the damn *something missing*—when he spoke, his voice rough around the edges, sexy as a touch.

"What the hell?"

She knew his eyes to be a shade of blue that was deeper than sapphire. But in the shadows where he stood, they looked black, sultrier than the summer night, smoky with new and unreadable mysteries.

For a moment she was absolutely paralyzed by his puzzled gaze on her. But then she came to her senses and lurched to her feet.

This was not how Brand Sheridan was going to see her after an eight-year absence! *Pathetic.*

Sophie scrambled toward the safety of the little hole in the hedge that she could squeeze through, and that she hoped he couldn't—or wouldn't. She would have made it, too, if she hadn't remembered the damned box.

She wasn't leaving it there for him to find, a box full of her romantic notions, as ridiculously unrealistic as a princess leaving a glass slipper for her prince to find.

The rest of the town might know she was pathetic, still think of her affectionately as their sweet geek—a romantic catastrophe now adding to her reputation—but she could keep it a secret from him.

She turned back, grabbed the box and then, disaster. She tripped over the hem of a dress she had left too long in the hope it would make her look taller and more graceful as she glided down the aisle.

Sophie crashed to the ground, face-first, and the box sailed from her hands and spilled its contents to the wind. Papers and pictures scattered.

He moved toward her before she could find her breath or her feet.

And then his hand was on her naked shoulder, and he turned her over. And she gazed up into his face and felt the sizzle of his hand on the tender flesh of her shoulder, whatever had been missing between her and Gregg bubbled up so sweetly in her it felt as if she had drunk a bottle of champagne.

He stared down at her, his brow furrowed, his expression formidable and almost frightening. *This was Brand?*

And then the hard lines of his face softened marginally. Puzzlement knitted the line of dark brows. "Sweet Pea?"

She drank in his face. Still a face that could stop the sun, but a new dimension to it, the lines cast in steel, his eyes colder, she thought, dazed. *Something in his expression that had never been there. Haunted.*

His hand moved from her shoulder, he brushed a smudge of something from her cheek.

It would be way too easy to mistake the leashed strength in those hands for all kinds of things that it wasn't.

Just taking care of his awkward-situation-prone little neighbor, as always. Picking her up and dusting her off after yet another catastrophe. Her love for him giving her an absolute gift for clumsiness, for downright dumbness, for attracting mishap and mayhem.

She closed her eyes against the humiliation of it. The truth was, in those tender adolescent years after he had gone away and joined the military, she had imagined his return a million times. Maybe a zillion. The day he would come home and *discover* her. Not a gawky teenager with not a single curve, unless you counted the metallic one of the braces on her teeth.

But a woman.

She had imagined his voice going husky with surprise. Delight. *Sophie, you've become so beautiful.*

But of course, *nothing* ever went as she imagined it.

"Sweet Pea, is that you?"

She allowed herself just to look up at him, to drink in his scent and his presence and his mystery.

Brand Sheridan had always been crazy sexy. It wasn't just that he was breathtakingly good-looking, because many men were breathtakingly good-looking. It wasn't just that he was built beautifully, broad and strong, at ease with himself and his body, because many men had that quality, too.

No, there was something else, unnamable, just below the surface, primal as a drumbeat, that made something in Sophie Holtzheim go still.

If he had ever gone through an awkward teenage stage, she had been blind to it. Since the day she had moved in next door, Sophie had worshipped her five-years-older neighbor.

Laughter-filled, devil-may-care Brand Sheridan had always been too *everything* for sleepy Sugar Maple Grove. He'd been too restless, too driven, too adventure-seeking, too energetic, too fast, too impatient.

His father, the town doctor, had been conventional, Brand had defied convention. And his father's vision for him.

To Dr. Sheridan's horror, Brand had defied the white-collar traditions of his family, quit college and joined the military. He had left this town behind without so much as a glance back.

Sophie had rejoiced with his parents when he had returned safely to the United States after a tour of duty abroad.

When had that that been? Five years ago? No, a little longer, because he had been overseas when her parents had died. But, in truth, Brand had never really returned.

He had not come home, and to his mother's horror, before they had really even finished celebrating his safe return from the clutches of danger, he had been recruited into an elitist international team of warriors known as FREES. For the most part, he lived and trained overseas or on the west coast. He worked in the thrum of constant threat, in the shadows of secrecy.

In those years away, Sophie was aware he had met his parents in California, in London, in Paris. She knew he occasionally showed up for family gatherings at his sister, Marcie's, house in New York.

It had, over the years, become more than evident Brand Sheridan had left Sugar Maple Grove behind him, and that he was never coming back. He'd been unconvinced of the joys of small-town life that Sophie had once outlined in her national-speech-competition talk, "What Makes a Small Town Tick."

Still, the whole town had felt the shock of it when Brand had not even returned home for his mother's funeral. The framed picture of him staring out sternly from under the cap of a United States Marine uniform had disappeared from Dr. Sheridan's mantel.

"Brandon," Sophie said, suddenly flustered, aware she had studied him *way* too long. She used his full name to let him know she was prepared to see him as an adult and that they could leave the endearment, *Sweet Pea*, behind them.

"I wasn't expecting you." As soon as the words were out of her mouth, she regretted them. She *always* had a gift for saying exactly the wrong thing around him, as awkward as the Sweet Pea she was anxious to leave behind her.

Of course she wasn't expecting him! She was in a wedding dress at midnight! If she'd been expecting him, what would she be wearing?

Well, a wedding dress would be nice, a part of her, the hopelessly romantic part of her she'd set out to kill tonight, said dreamily.

She shivered at the thought of Brand Sheridan as a groom. Glanced into the hard planes of that face and tried to imagine them softening with tenderness.

The tenderness she'd heard in his voice when he'd called her after the death of her parents. *Aww, Sweet Pea...*

That had been sympathy, Sophie reminded herself sternly. It was not to be mistaken for that stupid *something* she had tossed her life away for!

"Expecting someone else, if not me?" he asked.

He held out his hand to her, and she took it, trying to ignore another jolt of shimmering, stomach-dropping awareness as her hand met the unyielding hardness of his.

He pulled her to her feet with effortless strength, stood there regarding her.

"No, no," she said. "Just, uh, burning some urgent rubbish."

"Urgent rubbish," he said, and a hint of a smile tickled across the hard line of his lips.

She was suddenly aware that she truly, at this moment, was living up to Mrs. Hamilton's assessment of her as pathetic. A simple touch, her hand enfolded in his, not even a romantic gesture, made her feel things she had not felt through her entire engagement.

And that was before she added in the fact she had not had a decent haircut in months. Or put on a lick of makeup. Of all the people to catch her in her wedding dress, conducting ritualistic ceremonies at midnight, did it have to be him?

Did it have to be Brand Sheridan?

He let go of her hand as soon as she was steady on her feet, and turned away from her. He began to pick up the scattered wedding-dream debris, and shoved stuff back in the box, Sophie saw thankfully, without showing the least bit of interest in what that stuff was.

Sophie could have made her getaway through the hedge, but she found herself unwilling to abandon the box, and even though she knew better, unwilling to walk away. She felt as if she had not had a drink for days and he was clear water.

Days? No, longer. Months. Years.

And so she drank him in, thirstily. Part of her parched with a sense that only he could quench it, even though she despised herself for thinking that.

He was more solid than he had been before, boyish sleekness had given way to the devilishly attractive maturity of a man: broadness of shoulder, deepness of chest. And that was not all that had changed.

His dark hair was very short, his face clean-shaven. His dress was disappointingly conservative, even if the short-sleeved golf shirt did show off the breathtaking muscles of his biceps and forearms.

She felt a sharp sense of missing the boy who had walked away from here and not looked back. That boy of her memory had been a renegade. Back then, he had gone for black leather jackets and motorcycles.

To his mother's consternation, he had favored jeans with rips in them—sometimes in places that had made Sophie's adolescent heart beat in double time. His dark hair had been too long, and he'd always let a shadow of stubble darken the impossibly handsome planes of his face.

Now his hair was short, his face completely clean-shaven. There was the hard-edged discipline of a soldier in the way he held himself—an economy of movement that was mouth-dryingly masculine, graceful and powerful.

But, then her eyes had caught on the tiny hole in his ear.

Whoo, boy. Really too easy to imagine him as a pirate, legs braced against a tossing sea, powerful arms folded over the broadness of his chest—naked, she hoped—his head thrown back, welcoming the storms that others cringed from—

Stop, she pleaded with herself. God, she had been a reasonable person for years now! Years. She had almost married the world's most reasonable man, hadn't she?

And here he was, Brand Sheridan, wrecking it all. Wrecking her illusions, making her see she was not a reasonable person at all.

And probably never had been.

CHAPTER TWO

"Do you have a pieced ear?" Sophie gasped, despite the fact she had *ordered* herself not to ask. More of her gift for getting it *so* wrong. It would have been so much better if she hadn't noticed, or at least pretended not to have noticed!

Brand frowned, apparently not pleased that she had noticed, either. "I did," he said, touched the lobe of that ear, let his hand fall away. But his voice invited no more questions, even while his ears invited nibbling....

Ever since she'd been voted "girl least likely to nibble earlobes" in her high-school annual, she'd thought about what it would be like to do just that. Not that she had ever let those raucous boys who had voted for her know that.

Let them think she was prim and stiffly uptight. They would have teased her even more unmercifully if they'd guessed at her secret romantic side.

She'd never had any urges to nibble Gregg's ears. She'd been pleased that he had brought out her *reasonable* side. But of course, the *something missing* had reared its ugly head, and it probably had something to do with the forbidden temptations of earlobe-nibbling.

Especially ones that bore the mark of a piercing!

Sophie reminded herself she did not even know this man who shared the shadows with her at the moment.

He was not the same man who had called her all those years ago, on the worst night of her life, his voice alone penetrating the darkness, husky with pain. *Aww Sweet Pea*...she needed to remember that.

Brand Sheridan was not the same man who had left here. Really, he'd only been a boy when he left. And she'd been a girl, a carefree one, her biggest trouble trying to leave her nerdy reputation behind her. She'd been blissfully unaware of the tragedies that awaited her, both her parents killed in a terrible accident when she was eighteen.

Brand, apparently oblivious to her fascination with his earlobes, picked up another paper, stuffed it in the box, scanned the yard and then turned back to her.

Now, she could see it was the look in his eyes, not his earlobes, that was the most changed. Sapphire-dark, the firelight winked off that impossible shade of blue, deep and mysterious as the ocean.

Back then, she remembered, there was an ever-present sparkle of mischief in them, laughter never far away, a devil-may-care grin always tickling around the edges of that too-sexy mouth.

Now his eyes were wary. And weary. A shield was up in them that Sophie somehow doubted he ever let down.

And his mouth had a stern line etched around it, as if he no longer smiled, as if the mischievous boy who had caught the neighbor's snotty Siamese cat and tied a baby bonnet on it before releasing it was banished from him somehow. In the place of that boy was a warrior, *ready* for things that were foreign to the citizens of this tiny town.

She wanted to touch the firm line of that mouth, as if

she would be able to feel the smile that had once been there. She wanted to say, *Brand, what's happened to you?*

Thankfully, sensible Sophie took charge before she made a complete fool of herself.

"Thank you, Brandon," she said, and wrested the box from him. Realizing she sounded stiffly formal, she added, "I'll remember you in my will."

Stop it, she pleaded with her inner geek. *Please just stop!*

But the tiniest of smiles teased the hard line around his mouth, and she found herself surprised and pleased that he remembered the line she always thanked him with when he had come to her defense.

"That's a line from my past," he said wryly.

"I did have a gift for getting into scrapes," she admitted reluctantly.

"I remember. What was the name of that kid who chased you home after the game at Harrison Park?"

"I don't remember," she said stiffly, though of course she remembered perfectly.

"Ned?"

"Nelbert," she offered reluctantly, even though it was an admission she might remember after all.

"Why was he chasing you?"

"I don't remember."

"Just a sec. I do!"

Please, no.

"You told him he was more stupid than a dog who chased skunks," Brand recalled, "Right?"

"I thought because I'd learned to say it in Japanese I could get away with it. As it turned out, tone was everything."

And just when she had thought she was dead, because she had made it all the way home and no one had been there, Nelbert practically breathing down her neck, Brand had stepped out of the shadows off his porch. He had folded his arms across his chest, planted his legs and smiled, only it hadn't really been a smile.

He hadn't done anything else, nor had to. Nelbert had stopped dead, and skulked off, not even daring to glare at her. Nelbert had never tried to even the score again, either.

"Japanese," Brand said, and gave a rueful little shake of his head. "You were always a character."

A character. Thanks. I'm hoping for my own comic-book series.

"So, what are you doing in my dad's yard in your—" He studied her intently for a minute. "—is that a nightgown?"

"Oh, you know, just doing what comes naturally. Being a character."

See? Just when she thought she had nothing to be grateful for, Sophie had been saved from getting married in front of the whole town in a dress that people would say looked like a nightgown, her gift for getting things exactly wrong not as far in her past as she might have hoped.

She continued brightly, "I was just doing a little burning. Some rubbish." She began to edge her way toward the hole in the hedge. Men like Brand Sheridan were like drugs. He could make her forget what she'd come out here to do—say good-bye to romantic notions.

Not to start believing in them all over again. A man like him could make a woman like her—determined to face the world, strong, realistic, independent—capitulate to a weaker side. A side that leaned toward the fantastic—pirates, earlobe nibbling, or the worst fantasy of all: *forever*.

"You're burning rubbish at—" He glanced at his watch,

frowned. "—midnight?" He frowned and shot a glance at the house. "Does my dad know you're out here?"

"He's away." She edged closer to the hedge. "Didn't he know you were coming?"

Dr. Sheridan was busy wooing Sophie's grandmother, who had come from Germany after Sophie's parents had died, reading between the lines of Sophie's proclamations she was just fine, *knowing*, as only a grandmother knew, that she wasn't *fine*, trying to fix it with schnitzel and *kaese spechle*.

Magic foods that had helped, if not healed. Helped not just her, but Dr. Sheridan after Mrs. Sheridan had died so suddenly.

This weekend her grandmother and Brand's father were taking in Shakespeare at the Park in Waterville, the next town over. They were staying the night.

Sophie had not enquired about whether their accommodations were single or double. She didn't want to know, and they were always so sweetly discreet. But it certainly didn't feel like her place to update Brand on his father's love life.

"I thought I'd surprise him," Brand said.

There was something in the way he said that, with a certain flat grimness in his tone, that made her think Brand probably knew his picture had been taken off the family mantel.

She should remember that when his scent was acting like a drug on her resolutions. He was a man who couldn't even come home for his own mother's funeral. His father had not said *couldn't*, but *wouldn't*.

"Your dad will be home tomorrow." She remembered the lateness of the hour. "Or is that today? I guess it is today, now. Sunday. Yes."

He'd always had this effect on her. Smart, articulate

woman manages to make a fool out of herself every time she opens her mouth.

I'm not fifteen, her inner voice shouted. Out loud, she said pleasantly, "And I'm sure he will be surprised. Well, good—"

The wind picked that moment to sail a wayward wedding picture cartwheeling across the ground in front of him. He stooped, snagged it, straightened and studied it.

Handed it to her silently.

It was a picture of the inside of a stone chapel, with a bride kneeling at the altar alone, her dress spilling down stone stairs.

A bride alone. At the time the picture had seemed blissfully romantic, with a serenity to it, a sacredness. In light of her new circumstances, the bride looked abandoned. She should have been more careful about the pictures she cut out.

Sophie crumpled it and threw it in the box.

"Rubbish," she reiterated proudly.

He studied her for a long, stripping moment. It occurred to her he might be able to tell she'd been crying. She hoped not!

"That's not a nightgown, is it, Sweet Pea?" His voice was suddenly soft, impossibly gentle for a man with such hard lines in his face and such a cynical light in his eyes.

Just like that, he was the man who had called her the night her parents had been killed, getting her through the hours that followed, *awww, Sweet Pea.*

She steeled herself against his pirate charm.

"No," she said and tilted her chin proudly, "It's not a nightgown."

"Are you going to up and get married?" he asked, and

his tone had that familiar teasing note in it, a note that did not match the new lines in his face.

Had Brand and his father become that estranged? That Dr. Sheridan didn't even share the town news with him? The gossip, everyone knowing everyone else's business, who was having babies and who was getting married—and who was splitting up—was part of what made a small town tick!

Still, there was something refreshing, freeing, about being with the only person in her world who didn't know her history. Who wasn't sending her sideways looks, loaded with sympathy now that Gregg had chosen another.

"I'm marrying the mystery of the night," she told him solemnly. "It's an ancient ceremony that dates back to the worship of goddesses."

He contemplated her for a moment, and she had that feeling again. Why did she always feel *driven* to say foolish things around him?

But then he rewarded her with a smile that, ever so briefly, chased the dark shadow from his eyes.

"Sweet Pea, you were always an original."

"Yes, I know, an original *character*."

"Do you know how rare that is in the world?" The sadness in his eyes had returned.

She didn't. She wanted to invite him to the fire so he could tell her what a good thing it was. Wanted to chase the shadows from his eyes and make him laugh. And feel his touch again.

He was a weakness in a life she was determined to make about strength and independence. If she really practiced ancient ceremonies, which she didn't, Brand Sheridan's sudden arrival would surely be interpreted as a test of her commitment.

"Good night," she said firmly, and pushed her way,

finally, through the gap in the prickly hedge. She felt sick when the dress caught, somewhere high up the back of her rib cage, the snagging sound loud against the quiet of the night.

She froze, then pulled tentatively, but she was caught, and even though she reminded herself she didn't need this dress anymore, she couldn't bring herself to risk wrecking it by yanking free.

Now what? Set down the box to free up her hands so she could untangle the dress? Even bending to set down the box was probably going to damage the dress further.

She cast a look over her shoulder, hoping Brand had departed at her firm good-night. But, oh no, he stood there, arms folded over the solidness of his chest, watching her, amusement playing with the stern cast of his features.

Around him, everything always went wrong. Would a dignified departure have been too much to ask for?

Sophie backed up a half step hoping that would release the twig caught in her dress. Instead she heard a brand-new snagging sound at her waist.

How was it she had managed to get through the hedge the first time without incident?

Now she was afraid to move at all in case she tangled the dress further in the twigs. She could throw down the box, but what if its contents scattered *again?*

It seemed like an hour had passed as she contemplated her options. A gentleman would have figured out she needed help.

But Brand, black sheep of his family, was no gentleman. That was evident when she slid him another look.

He was *enjoying* her situation. His shoulders were actually shaking with mirth, though he was trying to keep his expression inscrutable.

"Could you give me a hand?" she snapped.

She would have been better off, she realized, too late, to rip the dress or throw down the box. Because she had invited him in way too close.

He shoved through the hedge, oblivious to the prickles and the fact the gap was way too small to accommodate him. He stood at her shoulder, pressed close. For the second time, the scent of him, warmly, seductively masculine, filled her nostrils. Now, she could also feel the warmth of his breath tickling the nape of her neck, touching the delicate lobe of her ear.

She was instantly covered in goose bumps.

Naturally, he noticed!

"Are you cold, Sophie?" he asked, his voice a rough whisper that intensified the goose bumps.

"Frozen," she managed to mumble, "it's chilly at this time of night."

That declaration gave her an excuse to shiver when his hand touched her arm, heated, Brand branding her.

He laughed softly, not fooled, all too certain of his charm around women. And she was absurdly, jealously aware this was not the first time he had handled the intricacies of women's clothing.

He might have been touching a wounded, frightened bird, his fingers on her tangled gown were so exquisitely gentle.

Experienced, she told herself. Brand Sheridan had been out of her league before he had made a career of being an adventurer. Now, every exotic world he had visited was in his touch.

"There," he said.

She gritted her teeth. "I think I'm caught in one more place. Left side. Waist."

His breath moved away from her ear, she felt his hand trace the line of her waist in the darkness.

With a quick flick of his wrist that came both too soon and not nearly soon enough, she felt him free her. She dashed away without saying thank you and without looking back.

But his chuckle followed her. "By the way, Sweet Pea, you can't marry the night. You promised you were going to wait for me."

Yes, she had. In one of those rash moments of late-night letter writing shortly after he'd left, full of the drama and angst and emotion a girl feels at fifteen and really never again, Sophie had promised she would love him forever. And had she done that? Thrown away the bird in hand for a complete fantasy she had sold herself when she was a young teen?

"Brand Sheridan," she called back, grateful for the distance and the darkness that protected her from his all-seeing gaze, "don't you embarrass me by reminding me of my fifteen-year-old self!"

"I loved your fifteen-year-old self."

A test. A black, star-filled night, a fire roaring in the background, her in a wedding dress, and Brand Sheridan *loving* her, even if it was who she used to be. Not that she should kid herself he'd had an inkling who she was, then or now. Or that what he so casually called love should in any way be mistaken for the real thing.

"You did not," Sophie told him sternly. "You found me aggravating. And annoying. Exceedingly."

His laughter nearly called her back to the other side of the hedge, but no, she was making her escape. She was not going to be charmed by him.

Time to get over it! Maybe it was a good thing Brand Sheridan had finally come home.

Maybe a person had to close the door on the past completely before they could have a hope for the future.

Maybe that's why things had not worked out between her and Gregg.

Ignoring the rich invitation of his laughter, and her desire to see if it could possibly erase whatever haunted his eyes, Sophie scuttled across her own backyard, and through the door of her house, letting it slam behind her.

Brand was aware, as he walked through the darkness back to the front of his father's home, that he felt something he had not felt in a long, long time.

It took him a moment to identify it.

And then he realized that his heart felt light. Sophie Holtzheim, Sweet Pea, was as funny as ever. The fact that it was largely unintentional only made it funnier.

"The goddess in the garden burning *urgent* rubbish *and* marrying the night," he muttered to himself, with a rueful shake of his head.

Still, there was a part that wasn't funny, Brand thought, searching over the casing of the front door for his father's hidden house key. Sweet Pea now looked like the goddess she had alluded to.

He wasn't even quite sure how he'd known it was her, she was so changed. He remembered a freckled face, a shock of reddish hair, always messy, constantly sunburnt and scraped. He remembered glasses, knobby elbows and knees, her hand coming up to cover a wide mouth glittering with silvery braces.

He remembered earnestness, a worried brow, a depth that sometimes took him by surprise and made him feel like the uneasy, superficial boy that he had been.

And no doubt still was.

He also remembered, with a rueful smile, she had been correct. He'd found her intensely irritating.

From the lofty heights of a five-year age difference

he had protected his funny little neighbor from bullies, rescued her from scrapes and tolerated, just barely, her crush on him.

For his first year in the military, her letters, the envelopes distinctive in her girlish hand and different colored inks, had followed him. At first just casual, tidbits of town news, a bit of gossip, updates on people they both knew, but eventually she'd been emboldened by the distance, admitting love, promising to wait, pleading for pictures.

He'd felt the kindest thing—and happily also the most convenient—had been to ignore her completely.

He'd been in touch with her only once, in the eight years since he had left here, a call when her parents had been killed in that terrible accident at the train crossing on Miller Street. She'd only been eighteen and he remembered wishing he could be there for her, poor kid.

Sophie had been part of the fabric of his life, someone he had taken for granted, but been fiercely protective of at the same time. He'd always had a thing about protecting Sophie Holtzheim.

He'd been overseas, at a base with one bank of telephones, when his mother had e-mailed him the news within minutes of it happening. He'd waited in line for hours to use one of those phones, needing to say *something* to Sophie. And instead of wise and comforting words coming out of his mouth, he'd held the phone and heard himself say, across the thousands of miles that separated them, *aww, Sweet Pea.*

How much he cared about his aggravating, funny nuisance of a neighbor had taken him by surprise, because if asked he probably would have claimed he was indifferent to her. That was certainly how he had acted the majority of the time. But on the phone that night, his heart felt as if it was breaking in two as he helplessly listened to her sob on the other end of the line. Brand felt as if he'd failed her by being a million miles away, instead of there.

Maybe it was always her eyes that had made him feel so attached to his young neighbor, despite the manly pretense of complete indifference.

Her eyes had a worried look that often creased her brow; they were hazel and huge. Even behind those glasses, they had been gorgeous way before the rest of her was. There had been something in them that was faintly unsettling and certainly older than she was: calm, as if she looked at a person and *knew* secrets about them they had not yet told themselves.

Seeing her tonight, *touching* her, he realized Sophie had grown into the promise of those eyes. And then some.

Her hair had lost the red and deepened to a shade of auburn that the firelight had licked at the edges of, making a man itch to touch it to see if it was fire or silk or a seductive combination of both.

He was not sure where freckles went when they went away, but there was no hint she had ever been a freckle-face. Her complexion now was creamy and perfect. Not that he had thought about it, but if he had, he would not have envisioned a grown-up Sweet Pea being quite so lovely.

Seeing her as a woman had been slightly unsettling. She had filled out that gown pretty nicely. If he hadn't realized just in time that it was Sweet Pea, he might have let his eyes drift to where the fabric clung to breasts that had been unfettered with anything as sinful as a bra.

But he was still the guy who had stood between her and her tormentors, and there had been as many who tormented her about her success with "What Makes a

Small Town Tick" as there had been those who were happy for her.

She'd never known when to back down, either. That girl had a gift for saying the wrong thing at the wrong time.

He'd even vetted her rare suitors, doing his best to scare them off, and given her unsolicited advice.

Sweet Pea, all men are swine.

Including you?

Especially me.

Brand had been the older brother she didn't have but badly needed.

Sweet Pea still lived next door. Didn't anything in Sugar Maple Grove ever change?

Yes, it did. Because she was not the same Sweet Pea he remembered. And he was not the same guy she thought she knew, either. He didn't feel like her older brother anymore.

He had not set foot in this town for eight years. Family occasions had long since moved to his sister's in New York, and his parents had visited him in California.

Brand suddenly remembered his mother's childlike enjoyment of Disneyland, how she would get off the Pirates of the Caribbean ride, and then get right back in line to go again.

Mom.

The light heartedness left him, and another feeling hit. Hard. On this porch where his mother had rocked and waited for him to come home, hours after the curfews he had always chaffed against, careless of her feelings.

He was aware he had managed to outrun his grief and his sense of failure toward his family until the exact moment he drove back into town, under that canopy of huge maples that lined the Main Street, past the tidy redbrick-fronted businesses, their bright awnings rolled up for the night.

The residential streets had been so quiet tonight, the sidewalks between the tree-lined boulevards and large grassy yards with their whitewashed picket fences completely empty.

He could sense people sleeping peacefully under those moss-covered roofs, curtains fluttering out of open, unlocked windows.

It was postcard-pretty small-town America. The place he had sworn his life to protect, and that, ironically, when he was young, he could not wait to get away from.

Now, standing on the porch of the house he had grown up in, searching for a key he knew would still be hidden in the same place, his mother's sweetness gathered around him.

He could practically taste her strawberry lemonade.

His father had made it clear he would never forgive him for not being at her funeral.

The words *deep cover* meant nothing to Dr. Sheridan, who did not consider a career chasing the world's bad guys to be in any way honorable.

There had been no explaining to his father that years of carefully laid work could have been lost if Brand had come home. Lives could have been endangered by breaking the cover.

"I don't want to hear your *excuses*," Dr. Sheridan had said the last time Brand had called.

"He's mad at you, anyway," his sister had told him, always pragmatic, when she had enlisted Brand to make this journey to their childhood home. "There's no sense his being mad at both of us, is there?"

Marcie had told Brand there had been an *incident*. A fire in the kitchen. An unattended frying pan.

His sister had some legitimate concerns and questions about whether their dad, seventy-four on his next birthday, who had never cooked for himself or looked after a house, should be starting now.

Brand, what if he's losing it? Then what?

That's what Brand was here to find out.

To do the job nobody else had the stomach for. Didn't that have a familiar ring to it? His whole adult life had been spent stepping up to the plates that wiser men stepped away from.

Finding the key, he went in. Without turning on lights, Brand went up the stairs and into a room with a steeply sloped roof that had once been his.

An open box inside the door was crammed full of Brand's football trophies and school photos—his grad picture was on the top—the one that had once been on the mantel.

He kicked off his shoes, flopped down, coughing slightly at the cloud of dust that rose out of the unused bedding. He closed his eyes. The whole house had a scorched smell to it that made him miserably aware of his mission.

He opened his eyes again, contemplated the flicker of light on the ceiling and realized the fire was still burning in the yard. He tried to reclaim the lightness he had felt earlier by thinking of his encounter with Sophie.

A thought blasted through his brain, unwelcome and uninvited.

Had Sweet Pea been crying?

He got it suddenly. Ah. She wasn't marrying the night. She'd just tried to distract him from the real story with her legendary cleverness. She was in his father's backyard at midnight burning wedding pictures in a wedding dress because somebody had broken her heart.

And it was only a sign of how tired he was, how the world he'd left behind was colliding with the one he'd made for himself, that instead of feeling sad for her, he felt oddly glad.

He didn't want Sweet Pea marrying anyone without his approval. It was as if eight years of separation didn't exist at all, and he was stepping back into the role he'd always assumed around her.

Big brother. Protector.

Only now, he thought, thinking of her huge eyes and the swell of her naked breast beneath the film of that sheer dress, he didn't exactly feel like a big brother. In fact, he could probably add himself to whomever or whatever he was protecting her from.

CHAPTER THREE

"I THINK I'll call the police," his father said, eyeing him from the bedroom door. "Break and enter is still against the law."

Brand turned over, winced at the light pouring into the room, eyed his father and then the clock. From his sister's reports he had expected his father to look older, frazzled, his white hair sticking up à la Albert Einstein.

Dr. Sheridan, in fact, had already combed his rather luxurious steel-gray hair, and looked quite dapper in dark pants, a crisp white shirt, a suit vest that matched the pants.

"It's not break and enter if you have a key," Brand said mildly. "Hi, Dad." It was nearly noon. Brand had slept for close to twelve hours.

"Humph. I guess you're the expert on all things criminal. If I called the cops, you'd probably flash your badge at them, wouldn't you? You'd probably have *me* arrested. Shipped off to an old folks' home. That's why you're here, isn't it?"

Whoo boy. Everything was going to be a fight—if he let it. Brand wasn't going to let it. There was absolutely no point telling his father he wasn't a cop, and he didn't have a badge. He was an *operative*. But he wasn't a doctor, and that's all his father really cared about.

"How are you, Dad?"

"That fire could have happened to anyone," his father said, defensively. "Your sister sent you here, didn't she?"

Brand felt relieved that his dad was obviously mentally agile enough to figure that out.

"Any chance of getting a cup of coffee?"

"Get your own damn coffee," his father snorted, "I'm having coffee next door."

"At Sophie's?" Brand asked, intrigued.

But his father didn't answer, gave him a dark look that let him know he was not included in coffee plans, and slammed the bedroom door.

That went well, Brand thought. On the bright side, Dr. Sheridan hadn't ordered Brand to get out of his house and never come back. Maybe there was something here they could salvage.

Unless his sister was right. If his dad was losing it, not capable of living on his own anymore, and if Brand was the one who had gathered the evidence, there would be nothing left to salvage.

"How did I get myself into this?"

He'd known he'd have to come home sooner or later, and, as it happened, he needed a place to be safe. God, if Sugar Maple Grove didn't qualify in spades. As if to confirm that, a church bell pealed in the distance.

Brand got up, stretched mightily, aware of how deeply rested he felt.

In four years deep undercover, assuming an identity, moving in a glitzy world of wealth and crime, a man lost something of himself. And he never quite slept. One eye open, part of him ever alert, part of him *hating* the life he lived, making people he would betray like him and trust him.

Well, not him. The role he played—Brian Lancaster—though who he was and who he pretended to be had begun to fuse together in ways he had not expected.

Now, having slept well, Brand felt more himself than he had felt for a long time. Or was it because he had seen the reflection of himself as he used to be, in Sophie's huge hazel eyes?

A funny irony that the place he couldn't wait to get away from might have something to give him back now, all these years later.

"Who could have predicted I would become a man who would treasure a good night's sleep more than most men would treasure gold?" he muttered ruefully to himself.

Brand showered and dressed, then moved downstairs, guiltily aware he was looking for evidence his father might be slipping.

Everything seemed to be in need of repairs, but Dr. Sheridan had never been gifted at things like that, faintly flabbergasted when Brand had shown an early knack with something so primitive as a hammer.

Brand's sister, Marcie, had said, vaguely: *if there's something wrong, you'll know. Mittens in the fridge, that kind of thing.*

"No mittens in the fridge," Brand said, opening the fridge door and peering inside. "No food, either." Did he report that to Marcie?

He went out the front door to his car—a little sports number he'd purchased before his Brian Lancaster assignment. Now, it seemed too much like a car Lancaster would have chosen, and he was aware of wanting to get rid of it.

Brand needed coffee. Did everyone still go for coffee

at Maynard's, morning coffee house, afternoon soda fountain and evening ice-cream parlor?

Brand was aware of a reluctance to see *everyone,* the chasms that separated his life from the life in this small town probably too deep to cross.

He never made it to the car.

"Young man. You! Come!"

An old woman, dapper in a red hat, was waving at him from Sophie's porch. He saw his dad and Sophie out there, too, and remembered Sunday brunch on the porch was always something of a pre-church tradition in Sugar Maple Grove.

He could smell the coffee from here and it smelled rich and good and added to that sense of coming home to small-town America.

He hesitated only for a moment, was drawn by curiosity to see Sophie in the light of day, and went through the gap in the hedge that separated the front lawns. The path between the houses was worn.

He registered, peripherally, a man trained to notice everything, that there was a lot of going back and forth between these two houses.

When his dad wasn't around, he would have to thank Sophie for looking in on him.

Sophie's porch was out of the American dream: deep shadows, dark wicker furniture with bright-yellow striped cushions, a gray-painted wood floor, purple-and-white petunias spilling color and scent out of window boxes.

And she was part of the same dream. Despite the fact his father and the old woman were there, Brand could see only Sophie. Somehow, in the years between them, she had gone from being a delightful little nerd to the all-American girl.

"Good morning, Sweet Pea," he said, taking the empty seat beside her.

"Don't call me that." Then, with ill grace, remembering her manners, "Brandon, this is my grandmother, Hilde Holtzheim."

"The pleasure is mine, but my granddaughter, she is not a sweet pee in the morning," the old woman said in heavily accented English, "More like a sour poop."

He could tell from the accent that Sophie's grandmother was German, and he almost greeted her in that language, one of three he spoke fluently thanks to countless hours in language school getting ready for overseas undercover assignments.

But before he could speak, Sophie did.

"Grandma! He doesn't mean that kind of pee! He's talking about a flower." Sophie was blushing. Brand could already feel that heavy place in him lightening.

"Oh." Sophie's grandmother's eyes widened. "He compares you with flowers?" she asked in German. "That's romantic!"

Maybe, he decided, it would be way more fun not to let on he spoke German. His father, colossally indifferent to any career choice outside of medicine, did not know his only son spoke any language other than English.

His decision paid off immediately when Hilde turned to Sophie and said in rapid German, "Ach. Gorgeous. You and him. Beautiful babies."

Sophie shot him a glance, and Brand kept his expression carefully bland, congratulated himself because it was obviously going to be so entertaining *not* to let on he spoke German.

"What did she say?" he asked Sophie innocently.

Today, Sophie wore a white T-shirt and shorts. Her hair, that amazing shade of mink browns and coppers mixed, was thick and sleep-rumpled. It was half caught up, half falling out of a rubber band. She didn't have a lick of makeup on.

She looked all of sixteen, but he knew she hadn't looked like this at sixteen because he had been the recipient of a picture taken at her sixteenth birthday party and she'd still been awkward then, duckling, pre-swan.

Now, it occurred to Brand that Sophie was going to be one of those women who came more and more into herself as she got older, but who would somehow look young and fresh when she was fifty.

"She said you don't look like the kind of man who would be interested in flowers." She shot Hilde a warning look.

"What kind of man do I look like?" he asked Hilde.

He was aware of liking sitting beside Sophie. She smelled of soap, nothing else, and he was surprised by how much he had missed something as simple and as real as a girl sitting on her front porch with no makeup and no perfume and her hair not styled.

She tried to hide her naked legs under the tablecloth, but before they disappeared, he noticed her toenails were painted candy-floss pink.

And he was struck again with a sense of having missed such innocence. In the world of Brian Lancaster, there had been no modesty. The types of women who were attracted to the wealth and power of the types of men he had been dedicated to putting in jail all aspired to be swimsuit models or actresses.

They were tanned, fit, artificially enhanced and wore lots of makeup and very little clothing. He did not think he had seen a natural hair color in four years. They had also been slickly superficial, materialistic and manipulative. For four years he had been surrounded by the new and international version of the old-fashioned mafia moll. His colleagues envied him the lifestyle he pretended at, but he had felt something souring in his own soul.

Brand had not even allowed himself to think of this world back here, of women who didn't care about flashy rings, designer clothes, parties, lifestyles so decadent it would have put the Romans to shame.

It occurred to him that he might have died of loneliness if he had allowed his thoughts to drift to someone like Sophie as he immersed himself deeper and deeper into a superficial world where people were willing to do any-thing—absolutely anything—to insure their place in it.

"You look like a man," Hilde said, starting in English and switching to German, "who would have a kiss that could change lead into gold."

"She says you look like a man with a good appetite," Sophie said, without missing a beat. "She wants you to eat something."

The table was loaded with croissants and muffins and homemade jams, fresh fruit, frosty glasses of juice—the simple meal seemed so good and so real after the world he had come from.

His stomach rumbled as the old lady in the red hat glared at her granddaughter, smiled approvingly at him, poured him a juice and then coffee.

"Eat," she insisted, and then in German, "A man like you needs his strength."

Sophie's German was halting. "Stop," she warned her grandmother, "be good."

"I'm supposed to be the old lady, not you," Hilde muttered, unrepentant. In German. "Look at his lips."

He was aware that Sophie looked, then looked away.

"Enough to make any woman," Hilde searched for the word in German, blurted out in English, "swine."

"Swoon," Sophie corrected her automatically, and then turned beet-red. "She says to tell you the raspberry jam is to swoon for. She means to die for."

The old woman was staring at his lips. "Yes, to die for."

He laughed. "That's mighty good jam."

Brand was aware his father had his arms folded stubbornly over his chest, not finding the hilarity all that hilarious. Brand dutifully looked at his father for any signs of malnourishment, given the condition of his fridge, but the elder Sheridan actually looked fleshier than Brand could ever remember in the past.

He turned his attention back to Sophie, who was still blushing. In the light of day, he was aware again how pretty she had become in a wholesome way, and how watching a girl like her blush was an underrated pleasure.

After the life he had lived undercover—infiltrating a gang of exceedingly wealthy and sophisticated weapons smugglers and currency counterfeiters—there was something about her wholesomeness—her ability to blush—that appealed to him, shocked him by making him yearn for a road not taken.

It occurred to him that maybe people should listen to the adage "you can't go home again" and not even try.

Because he could never be this innocent again. But maybe he could just enjoy this moment for what it was: simple, enjoyable, companionable.

He was aware, again, that that was the first time in years he had felt relaxed in a social situation.

Safe, he thought in a way only someone who lived with constant danger could appreciate. Once, he had hated how this place never changed.

Now, he thought, maybe a month here wouldn't be so bad after all.

He could see Hilde eyeing him with unremitting

interest, despite Sophie elbowing her in the ribs and warning her in soft German to quit staring.

"Your father tells me you're a secret agent," Hilde said, pushing Sophie's elbow away.

"No," he said firmly, though it surprised him his father had said anything about him, since he was persona non grata. "I belong to a military branch that was developed as an antiterrorism squad. I'm just a soldier."

"Very exciting," Hilde declared.

"Not really. Ninety-nine percent pure tedium, one percent all hell breaking loose."

"But you were under the covers?"

He saw Sophie, who was just beginning to recover from her last blush, turning a lovely shade of pink all over again beside him. In the world he had just come from, women didn't blush. And they said things a whole lot more suggestive than *you were under the covers.* Sophie's blush was so refreshing.

"I was. It's not as exciting as it sounds, believe me." The grandmother didn't look like she believed him, so he headed her off at the pass. "Sophie, I didn't have a chance to catch up with you last night. It's been what? Eight years? What do you do now?"

"Last night?" his father sputtered.

Brand could tell by Sophie's sudden slathering of marmalade on a croissant that what she had been doing last night was private to her. That instinct to protect her rose to the surface instantly.

"We ran into each other briefly when I arrived." He watched her out of the corner of his eye, saw her catch a breath of relief that the details of her secret ceremony by the fire were safe with him.

Still, if he remembered correctly, Sophie didn't even like marmalade.

"Oh," his father said, his tone crotchety.

Her grandmother looked disappointed, Sophie looked relieved. She took a bite of her croissant, and her eyes nearly crossed. She glared at the marmalade.

"I'll take that one," he said smoothly and passed her his own croissant and the jar of raspberry jam. "As I recall, your grandmother says this is the one to swine for."

He smiled at her to let her know he'd noticed she was rattled. And he raised an eyebrow evilly that asked if it was him that was rattling her.

But when she took a little nibble of the new croissant, ignoring the jam, and a crumb stuck at the corner of her mouth, he wondered just who was rattling whom.

"I work for the Historical Society," Sophie said, but reluctantly. "I'm sure you would find what I do exceedingly boring."

"It's not," his father rushed to her defense. "Sophie is our only paid employee at the Society. She's a whiz at organization. A whiz! She's going to write a book."

"Well, not exactly," she said swiftly, blushing sweetly *again*. "I'm going to gather material for a book. A collection of remembrances of Sugar Maple Grove during the Second World War. I won't really be writing it so much as selecting and editing."

It occurred to Brand that once upon a time he *would* have found Sophie's choice of work exceedingly boring. But having just spent four years around women who were ditzy, who thought it was cute to be dumb, he found himself intrigued by Sophie's career choice.

His father began to talk about the book with great relish—and considerable savvy.

Brand allowed himself to hope his sister was wrong,

and to sink deeper into the feeling of being somewhere good. And decent.

Then the mood suddenly changed. A bright-red sports car was slowing in front of the house, then, apparently having spotted the people on the porch, it pulled in.

Sophie had been starting to relax as Dr. Sheridan had waxed lyrical about Sugar Maple Grove's contribution to the war.

Now Brand was aware of her freezing, like a deer caught in headlights. Unless he was mistaken, she was getting ready to bolt.

"The nerve," her grandmother said, and then in German, "I'd like to cover him in honey and stake him out over an ant hill. Naked."

Brand, practiced at deception, never let on with so much as a flicker of a smile that he understood her perfectly. He watched, as did they all, as the man got out of his car.

If there was one thing Brand had gotten very good at spotting—and not being the least impressed by—it was wealth and all its trappings, the car, the designer sweater, the knife-pressed pants, the flash of a solid-gold pinkie ring.

"Mama's boy," his father hissed with disdain, and then shot Brand a look and muttered sulkily, "not that that's *always* such a bad thing."

But as he was reading the shift of mood at the table, it was Sophie that Brand was most aware of.

She had gone white as a sheet, and he could see tension in the curve of her neck, in the sudden locking of her fingers. She had hunched over as if she was trying to make herself smaller.

He had a memory from a long time ago. He and some friends shooting baskets at the riverside park where Main Street ended. Sophie had been walking home from school. She'd been thirteen, it had been after her speech in that national competition.

"Hey, metal mouth," some Main Street big shot had yelled at her. "What makes a small-town *hick?* You!"

Brand's eyes had flown to Sophie. He had seen her hunch over those books, trying hard to make herself invisible.

Brand had come out of that group shooting baskets and been across the street in a breath. He'd picked up that loser by his T-shirt collar, shoved him against the wall and held him there.

"Don't you ever pick on that girl again," he'd said, his quietness not beginning to hide his rage. "Or I'll make you into a small-town brick, pound you down to dust, make you into a little square and stick you on this wall forever. *Comprende?*"

Even then he'd had a certain warped gift for tackling things in a way that had made him a prime find, first for the United States Marine Corps and then for the unit he now served.

Through those organizations, Brand had become much more disciplined in his use of force, at channeling righteous fury to better purpose, at choosing when aggression was the appropriate response.

A frightened nod, and Brand had let the creep go, caught up to Sophie and slipped the books away from her.

"Put your head up," he'd told her. "Don't you ever let a dork like that control you, Sweet Pea."

No gratitude, of course.

She'd given him her snotty look, and said, "Brand Sheridan, don't even pretend you know what a dork is."

"It's a guy like that."

"It's a whale penis," she told him. And then she

blushed as if she had said or done something *really* bad, and surprisingly, he had blushed, too.

Now, sitting here beside her, he tried to think if he had blushed like that since then. Or at all. He doubted it.

But she still blushed.

Suddenly, Brand was aware she had flexed the muscles in her legs, just enough to push back slightly from the table, and he just knew she was going to bolt.

And that for some reason he couldn't let her. It was a variation of holding her head up high. He laid a hand on her arm, not holding her down, just resting his fingers lightly on her skin, his own hand completely still, willing his own stillness into her.

He felt her eyes on his face, but he didn't look at her, didn't take his eyes off the man who had made her shrink as if she was still the town brainiac carrying her books down Main Street, a target for every smart aleck with an opinion.

Brand was aware, even as he made himself go still, even as he let her see and feel only his stillness, that something in him coiled, *ready,* ready to protect her with his life if need be.

He didn't know exactly what was going on. But Brand knew whatever it was she couldn't run from this. Whoever Slick was coming up her front walk, Sophie shouldn't let him know he had that much power over her.

Why did he?

Slick came up the steps, sockless in designer sandals, and flashed them a smile made astoundingly white by perfect porcelain veneers.

"Dr. Sheridan. The *misses* Holtzheim."

He seemed unaware that no one looked happy to see him, that he would have to search long and hard to find a more unwelcoming group in Sugar Maple Grove.

He raised spa-shaped eyebrows at Brand, and put out his hand.

Brand half rose, took it, felt the softness, and squeezed just a little harder than might be considered strictly polite.

He did not return the smile, intensely aware of how stiff Sophie had become, her face rigid with pride, even as her hands gripped the tablecloth just out of view, white-knuckled.

"Brand Sheridan," he introduced himself.

"Oh, our war vet! What an honor, the hero returning to Sugar Maple Grove." His tone was *aw, shucks,* but Brand did not miss something faintly condescending in it. "I'm Gregg Hamilton."

Ah, the Hamiltons. Strictly white-collar. Old money. That explained the underlying disdain for the public servant.

"I think you might have gone to school with my brother, Clarence."

I think I might have taken a round out of him behind the school for having exactly the same snotty look on his face that you do.

Somewhere along the line the military had managed to channel all that aggression he'd visited on others. His father might not be willing to admit what a good thing that was, but Brand knew he was a better man for it.

Brand shrugged, letting nothing of his own growing disdain show in his face. This was what he was good at, after all, never letting on what he was really feeling.

"Sophie, Mama told me she dropped by yesterday. I just wanted to echo her invitation to come to Toni's and my engagement party. It would be so good if you came. I think you'll adore Antoinette. I'm hoping you'll be friends."

Hilde Holtzheim muttered something in German that was the equivalent of *go screw yourself, worm face.*

Suddenly Brand put together Sophie sitting in front of that fire last night in her wedding dress, burning all manner of wedding paraphernalia with her tension at the unexpected arrival of Slick Hamilton.

Surely, Sophie hadn't been going to marry this guy? Worm face?

But a quick glance at Sophie, trying so hard to retain her pride, a plastic smile glued across her face, confirmed it.

Not only had she been going to, it looked like she regretted the fact she wasn't! The little ceremony he'd interrupted at the fire pit last night was all beginning to make an ugly kind of sense now.

Well, that's what happened when you left a lovely hometown girl, innocent to the ways of the world, to her own devices for too many years. She had all kinds of room to screw up.

"Um," Sophie stalled, "I haven't checked the calendar yet. What day was it?"

Brand hated seeing her squirm, and he hated it that she was so transparent. The little worm could see just how badly he'd managed to hurt her—which was exactly the kind of thing that made little worms like him feel gleeful with power.

Gregg actually looked as if he was enjoying himself enough to pull up a chair and have a croissant with them!

Brand slid Sophie a look. Slick Hamilton wasn't the kind of threat you had to keep a hand free to get at your hidden holster for.

The look on her face reminded him of another time when he'd found her on this porch, alone, on the swing over there, listening to music drifting up from the high school. It had probably been sometime in that year before he left.

He'd been rushing somewhere, though it was funny how that somewhere had seemed so important at the time, but he couldn't remember it now.

But he could remember the look on her face as clearly as if it had happened yesterday.

"What's up?" he'd asked her.

"Nothing."

"Come on. You can't lie to me, Sweet Pea. How come you aren't at the school dance?"

"It's the Sweetheart Prom," she said and then her face had crumpled even as her chin had tilted proudly. "Nobody asked me to go."

At nineteen what did a guy know about tears except that he didn't want to be anywhere around them? A better person than nineteen-year-old him had been might have dropped his other plans, changed clothes, taken her to the prom.

But he hadn't. He had chucked her on the chin, told her proms rated pretty high on the stupid scale and gotten on with his own life.

Brand thought suddenly of all those cute letters she had sent him when he'd joined up, when he'd been posted overseas. His one-gal fan club. The envelopes always decorated with stickers and different colored inks, the contents unintentionally hilarious enough that he had read every word.

Never answered any, though. Not even once.

Had her younger self waited by the mailbox, hoping?

So, maybe it was because he regretted doing the right thing by her only when it was convenient for him back then that he made a decision now. He owed her something. A smidgen of decency, compassion in a hard world.

Being undercover had taught him to read situations,

and this one was obviously going as badly for her as it was going well for Gregg.

It felt like the most natural thing in the world to rescue Sophie.

"I think Sophie's going to have to say no," Brand said smoothly. "I'm only here for a little while. We don't want to waste any of our time together, do we, honey?"

He turned to look at her. She was no actress. If Slick Hamilton saw her mouth hanging open in shock, he'd know the truth.

And Brand didn't want him to know the truth. That she still loved Gregg Slick Hamilton. Or thought she did.

There was one way they both could find out.

He caught her cute little puffy bottom lip with his. Touched it, ran his tongue along it, made her world only about him.

It was probably a sin how much he liked it, but Brand was pretty sure his place was reserved in hell, anyway.

And the kiss accomplished exactly what he wanted.

Sophie was staring at him with wide-eyed awareness as if Gregg had vaporized into a speck in front of them. She licked her lip and her eyes had gone all smoky with longing.

Nope.

No matter what she might have convinced herself, she didn't love Gregg Hamilton and never had.

Not that Brand considered himself any kind of an expert on love.

Lips, though, that was quite another thing.

And he liked hers. A whole lot more than he'd expected to. His sense of having sinned deeply grew more acute.

"Well, Sophie," the swagger was completely gone out of Gregg's voice, "You know you're welcome to come. Bring your new friend with you."

The invitation was issued now with the patent insincerity of a man who saw something he'd been using to puff himself up disappearing before his eyes.

"We might just do that," Brand said easily.

Gregg got in his car and roared away, spitting stones as if they proved his testosterone levels were substantially higher than those of the next guy.

Brand committed to getting rid of his own sports car sooner rather than later.

"Were they to swine for?" Hilde demanded, mixing German and English.

"What?" Sophie asked, dazed.

"His lips!"

"No. Yes." She closed her eyes, gathered herself and then looked sternly at her grandmother. "Stop."

And then she turned to Brand. The dazed expression was completely gone from her face.

"What did you do that for?" she demanded.

He tried not to smile. The girl was transparent! It was written all over her that she was torn between yes and no, stop and go, hitting him or thanking him.

And it was written all over her that that kiss had rocked her tidy world in a way she would never want him to know. But then again, he didn't really want her to suspect it had rocked his, too.

"Your ex was just gloating over your discomfort at his arrival a little too much," he said quietly. "It bugged me."

"How did you know he was my ex?" she asked, aghast.

"I'm good at reading people," he said. He didn't add that it was a survival mechanism, that over the past few years his life had depended on that skill. "I'm glad about the ex part, Sophie. I didn't care for him much."

Her grandmother snickered with approval and Sophie shot her a quelling look.

"You only saw him for thirty seconds!"

"Like I said," he lifted a shoulder elaborately, "I have a gift for reading people."

"He looked like a good kisser," her grandmother insisted in German.

"Stop it!" Sophie said in English.

"Stop what?" Brand asked innocently.

She looked him straight in the face. "Stop rescuing me, Brand. I'm not fifteen anymore. I don't need your help with my personal affairs."

She blushed when she said *affairs* in just about the way she had when she'd said *dork* all those years ago, as if she was fifteen and had just used a risqué word. It was very sweet. *She* was very sweet. The kind of girl he knew nothing about.

She was right. He needed to stop rescuing her.

"It was just an impulse," he said. "It won't happen again."

She struggled to look composed. Instead she looked crushed.

"Unless you want it to," he couldn't resist tossing out silkily.

"I want it to," Hilde said, all in English. She reached across the table, touched Brand's hand. The mischief was gone from her eyes. "The whole town is whispering about my Sophie and *him*. I'd much rather they whispered about my Sophie and you."

CHAPTER FOUR

SOPHIE was still stuck on the *unless you want it to* part. Good God, she thought, she might be super-nerd of national-speech-contest fame, but of course she wanted it to. Happen again.

Sophie's lips were tingling from being kissed. She felt exactly like a princess who had been sleeping, the touch of those lips bringing her fully to life. She was aware some part of her had waited, longed for, wanted what had just happened since she was a scrawny flat-chested teen in braces and glasses.

His lips had tasted of passion and promises and of worlds she had never been to. Had not even known existed. Places she wanted desperately, suddenly, now that she did know of their existence, to visit.

Who wouldn't want more of that?

But, unless she was mistaken, Brand was enjoying her discomfort as much as he had just accused Gregg of doing.

Men!

Not that any man could hold a candle to her grand-mother, who apparently felt driven to share with Brand Sophie's closely guarded secret, that she was somehow becoming pathetic.

Sophie struggled through her embarrassment to remember her mission last night. To be free of all her romantic notions and nonsense.

She wasn't letting Mr. Brand Sheridan think she was still the starry-eyed fifteen-year-old she had once been.

She wasn't letting him know that one tiny ultra-casual brushing of lips had her ready to pack her bags and travel to unknown territory.

No! Sophie Holtzheim was taking back control and she was doing it right now. If Brand thought she was weak and pathetic and in need of his big, strong, arrogant self to rescue her, he'd better think again!

But Brand was looking at her grandmother, and suddenly he didn't look as if he was enjoying her discomfort over that kiss.

"It's a bad thing to lose face in a small town," he said quietly.

"Yes!" her grandmother crowed, delighted that he had understood her so completely.

"It would be good for Sophie to have a romance so heated it would make the whole town forget she ever knew him," Brand said thoughtfully

"Yes!" Her grandmother was beaming at his astuteness.

"Okay, I'll do it," Brand said, casually, as if he had agreed to his good deed for the day.

"Do what?" Sophie demanded.

"Romance you."

"You will not!"

"It will convince Gregg and the whole town that you're over him," Brand said with aggravating confidence, as if it was already decided.

"It's deceptive," Sophie said, and then realized that wasn't the out-and-out no that such an outlandish suggestion deserved.

"It could be fun," Brand said.

"I doubt that."

He raised an eyebrow at her in clear challenge. And then said, softly, "What are you afraid of?"

Now the only way she was going to show him she wasn't the least bit afraid of what had just happened between them was if she said yes. If she protested this idea too strenuously, he might know the truth: she *was* terrified of him and his ability to tear her safe little world so far apart she might never succeed in putting it back together.

But she had to admit there was something wonderfully seductive about saving face. It really was horrible to be branded as pathetic in a small town.

"Well, Brand," she said slowly, thoughtfully, "maybe we could have a little fake fling, under carefully orchestrated circumstances, of course."

"And let me guess," he said wryly, "you will be in charge of orchestrating the circumstances?"

If she was going to do this, and she had a sinking feeling that she was, she had to maintain absolute control over the situation.

He watched her, some challenge lighting the sapphire depths of his eyes until they sparkled like falling stars in a night sky. It was a look that could take away a woman's courage. It could intimidate. It could shake her belief that she could be in control of everything. Or anything.

If she allowed it to, that was, if she hadn't just vowed in front of her own burning dreams she was going to be a different kind of woman from now on.

The take-charge kind.

"How long are you going to be here, Brand?" she asked, keeping her voice all business.

"Maybe a month. I've got a lot of leave built up."

"A month?" his father sputtered, and then sent

Hilde an aggrieved look that Sophie easily interpreted as his son's presence in his life cramping his romantic ambitions.

Brand's eyes narrowed on his father for a moment, then he glanced at Hilde.

Hilde, naturally, looked unabashedly delighted at Brand's announcement of a long-term stay in Sugar Maple Grove. It was written all over her face that she was already planning Brand and Sophie's wedding.

And an adorable little house filled with babies. She hoped Hilde wouldn't say it, not even in German. Because her grandmother was known to say anything, commenting on Brand's kissing abilities being a case in point. What kind of grandmother did that?

Sophie slid Brand a look. The full force of his attention was back on her. Well, there was no denying he was a good kisser and would produce perfect babies. But if she wanted to stay in control of the perilous situation she was moving herself toward, she'd better not go there!

"What are you going to do here for a month?" Dr. Sheridan asked sulkily. "You'll be bored in three days. Ha. Maybe in three hours."

Once, Sophie knew, Brand would have risen to the bait, argued whether what his father said was true or not, and it probably was. He had been hotheaded, impulsive, impatient.

Now, there was something new in him, something coolly disciplined that made him both harder to read and more intriguing.

Brand just shrugged and said, "It'll probably take me a month to fix everything in your house that is broken."

She looked between the two men, and saw it wasn't just the house that needed fixing.

Sophie could feel her head starting to ache. Those Sheridan men were probably going to need her help to navigate the minefield between them.

Great. She was going to have to do that while never letting Brand know how that kiss had rattled her world. How him sitting beside her on a sleepy Sunday morning made her feel aware and alive.

But, she reminded herself, this was exactly what she needed. To prove to herself she wasn't fifteen anymore, the mere whiff of him enough to make her waste her life dreaming of happily-ever-afters. No, she was all grown up now and immune to his charm, considerable as that was.

Once she did that, longing for things that didn't exist wouldn't have the power to ruin her life anymore.

She could be a realist, dismiss that longing for *something*. It wouldn't be there, like a villain waiting in the wings, ready to rain disaster on her well-planned future and life.

But she knew she was playing with fire. Because that *something* was exactly what she had tasted on his lips.

Walk into it, girl, she ordered herself. *If you want to play with fire, walk straight into the flame.* There would be nothing like a dose of reality to kill her fantasies forever.

"Well, Brand," she said, taking that mental leap off Blue Rock, "since you're going to be here, you might as well help me out. It's true, this whole town thinks I'm pining away for my ex-fiancé, Gregg, who is about to become officially engaged to someone else."

"Are you?" he asked softly.

"Of course not!" But she could feel a blush rising up her neck as she said it, and she could see she had not convinced him.

She took a deep breath, walked straight into the fire. "So, I'll accept your offer. Yes, you can pretend to be my beau."

It was like falling straight off a cliff. And no one hated heights more than she did!

"Beau?" he said, and then laughed. "Who uses a word like that in this day and age? I think you've been spending just a little too much time at the Historical Society, Sweet Pea."

"You are every bit as annoying as I remember!" she said, exasperated. It was hard enough for her to keep her dignity while accepting his offer.

"You *never* thought I was annoying," he said with the silky and aggravating confidence of a man who, unfortunately, women did not find annoying. Ever.

"Remember the time you said you were going to the library and I gave you my books to return and you didn't?"

"I wasn't really going to the library," he said.

"Whatever. Annoying. Six dollars in fines."

"Your only brush with the law?"

She ignored him. "And how about the time you showed up at my door with a kitten two minutes before I was supposed to be leaving for band camp?"

"You *loved* that kitten," he said, with a grin.

She had. The gift had *melted* her.

"That's not the point. The point is that I was late for band camp, and so I didn't get the instrument I wanted, and I had to play the tuba for a whole week and it was your fault."

"Band camp is for nerds."

"My point exactly," she said, triumphantly. "You are annoying! Supremely! You will have to try and keep that in check as we conduct our—" She couldn't bring herself to say romance. "—arrangement."

"Do you still play the tuba?" he asked sweetly. "Didn't you send me a recording? When I was in basic?"

Sophie could feel her face getting very hot. "I didn't!"

"Uh-huh. A tuba solo. A love song."

"It wasn't a tuba," she said petulantly. "Clarinet. My instrument of choice."

He raised a wicked, wicked eyebrow at her.

How could he do this? *Instrument* was not a dirty word!

"Never mind," Sophie said. "I just realized how rash it was to agree to this. I'm not sure I'm desperate enough to have you for my beau, even temporarily."

"Aw, shucks," he said. "Just when I was starting to think it might be fun. Like porcupine-wrestling in my birthday suit."

He had inserted that reference deliberately to see if he could make her blush again.

And damn him, he could.

"Are you backing out?" she demanded.

"No, I think you are."

"I'm not!"

"Ha," Dr. Sheridan muttered, "I'd be interested to see if the all-important Brand Sheridan, secret agent, would do anything as selfless as help an old neighbor so she could hold her head up high again. Trust me, Sophie, it's not in my son's nature to do the decent thing."

Sophie felt shocked at the doctor's bitter tone, and she saw Brand flinch as if he'd been struck.

She had found the bantering back and forth between her and Brand edgy, but playful, dangerously invigorating.

Now the tension that leapt in the air between him and his father was painful and tangible.

But again, the young man who would have risen to the bait, defended himself or argued, was not part of who Brand was now. Instead he replied, disciplined patience in his voice, "I'm just a soldier. I do what I'm told, when I'm told. I was on an undercover assignment. I was told I wouldn't be granted leave. Period."

"Whatever," his father said.

"If I could have been here, I would have."

"Whatever," his father said again.

"And if Sophie agrees, we'll do this thing."

She felt the flutter of her heart. It wasn't a good idea. To play a charade for the whole town was a stupid, impulsive idea that fell solidly into the category of really dumb things that she always did around him.

But could she walk away from giving Brand a perfect opportunity to redeem himself a tiny bit in his father's eyes while he was here?

It would help her, it would help him.

Even now, he and his father were eyeing each other balefully.

And she felt compelled to insert herself between them, to ease the tension.

"I'll do it," she announced decisively.

"Oh, goody," her grandmother said.

"Oh, brother," his father said.

"Oh," Brand said, then, "great." Spoken with the macho bravado of a man who had been chosen from many to diffuse a bomb.

"Let's talk romance," Sophie suggested brightly. "I'll come up with a plan. A few highly visible activities: ice cream at Maynard's, maybe a bike ride or two, an appearance at Blue Rock and then—ta-da—you and I at the engagement party."

Brand watched her talk, ruefully aware she was trying to ease the tension between him and his father. She'd

been like that as a kid, too. Always wanting everything
to look like a Norman Rockwell painting.

Sugar Maple Grove lent itself to that.

But now Sophie was not a kid. Not if those lips had
spoken the truth about her, and he was pretty sure they had.

He was also ruefully aware that, despite her engagement and the promise of those lips, Sophie still seemed
to be a sweet geek in the romance department. A plan?
What kind of romance had a plan?

A fake one, he reminded himself sternly.

Brand was struck by a tingling awareness along the
back of his neck. It was his sharply honed instinct. It
always warned him when danger was near.

He had done many, many dangerous things.

But he doubted any of them were going to hold a
candle to pretending to be Miss Sophie Holtzheim's *beau.*

Why had he agreed to this?

Partly because he couldn't resist protecting Sophie.
It seemed that's what he had been born to do, protect.

It was going to be a long, hot month in Sugar Maple
Grove, and a man couldn't be faulted for finding a way
to entertain himself.

His father, with one last look at him, not friendly,
shoved back his chair. "I'm going to be late for church."

"Oh, that time already?" Hilde said in English, and
in German, "We'll leave you two alone, Sophie. Do
something romantic, for God's sake."

In a flurry of activity his dad and Hilde left and it
was suddenly so quiet he could hear birds singing and
bees buzzing.

He waited to see if Sophie would do something romantic. Sophie, predictably, did nothing of the sort.

"Don't you have a girlfriend who's going to object

to this?" she asked. It sounded like an effort—albeit a weak one—to find a way out.

"I don't have a girlfriend," he said. "This job busts people up. It's too hard on the ones left behind. I was undercover for four years. Can you imagine what that would do to a woman?"

"The right one would be okay with it," she said with an edge of stubbornness. "It's not just what you do. It's who you are."

"Well, who I am can't just drop everything for the birthday or wedding anniversary. You get in too deep to be pulled out. Sometimes you have to pretend to have a wife or a girlfriend. Another agent plays the role. How does the woman waiting at home handle that?"

"Badly," she guessed.

"Exactly."

"I guess that overcomes the girlfriend thing."

"I guess it does."

"If we do this right," she said, "maybe your father won't be quite so antagonistic toward you."

On the other hand, Brand thought, if he did more damage than good, he would confirm his father's worst thoughts about him.

"I don't understand why he's not proud of you," Sophie said.

He didn't like it that she cut so quickly to his own feelings. Why was it a man never quite got over that longing to be something good in the eyes of his father? To make his family proud?

"There was only one way to make my father proud of me," he said, "and I didn't do it. I didn't go to medical school and become a doctor willing to take over the Sugar Maple Grove General Practice one day."

"I still remember how shocked your parents were when you quit college and joined the military."

"My dad can trace eight generations of Sheridans. The men are doctors, professors, writers. And then along came me. I couldn't fit the mold he made for me."

"But the marines?"

"A recruiter at college found me on a climbing wall and asked if I'd ever considered making a living doing something like that. He made the whole thing sound irresistibly exciting."

"And has it been?"

Brand was aware it was so easy to talk to Sophie. "It's been pretty much what I told your grandmother. Ninety-nine percent tedium, one percent all hell breaking loose."

Sophie smiled. "And you live for that one percent. Adrenaline junkie."

"You know, that's the part my mom and dad never understood. The military is a good place for an adrenaline junkie. I've always been attracted to adventure. I've always needed the adrenaline rush. Left to my own devices, especially in my younger years, that could have gotten me in a lot of trouble. I needed to balance my love of height and speed with discipline and skill.

"But my dad can't forgive me my career choice. We were a long way down the road of not seeing eye to eye even before I missed my mom's funeral."

"Was there really no way for you to come home, Brand? None?"

He shook his head. "You have to understand how deeply I was in and how long it took me to get there. Word of my mom's death reached me via a quick and risky meeting with my handler—that's your contact with the real world. The less you see anybody from that world, the better.

"At that point in the operation, I had to assume everything was suspect, everything was listened to, everything was watched. One wrong step, one wrong breath could have gotten people killed, could have blown nearly four years of work.

"What I said to my dad was true. I'm basically a soldier. I take orders. Even if it had been my call, which it wasn't, I wouldn't have jeopardized the team. Couldn't.

"And I'll tell you what else I couldn't have done— risked someone following me back here, knowing anything about this place or the people in it, retribution for what I was about to do raining down on the innocent."

Her eyes were wide. "Did you ever tell that to your father?"

"He doesn't listen long enough." Brand was surprised by just how much he'd told Sophie. He usually didn't talk about work. He usually carried his burdens alone.

"Are you in danger now?" she asked, always intuitive.

But he'd said enough, there was no sense scaring her. He sidestepped the question. "My identity will be protected, even in the coming court cases. I'll be kept pretty low-profile for a long time."

His father didn't know about that kind of world, and neither did Sophie Holtzheim. If he told them all the details, if they fully understood the danger, they might feel the kind of helpless fear that tore apart the ones who stayed at home.

Better his father be angry than that.

And her? He could never subject someone as sweet and sensitive as Sophie to what he did for a living. Was this brief tangling of their lives—him entertaining himself at her expense—going to hurt her?

It was going to be just like being undercover. Get the

job done, no emotional attachment, keep mental distance. *Pretend.*

He looked at Sophie, so adorable in her earnestness. Pretense around someone so transparent, so genuine, seemed wrong. Still, it bugged him that she wasn't able to hold her head high, so he listened without comment as she outlined her plans for a romance.

Ice cream. A bike ride or two. Blue Rock.

Again, he was struck by the innocence of it all. He felt a flicker of trepidation about his ability to play the role she was outlining. But he didn't let on.

"Sure," he agreed to all her plans when she finally stopped and looked at him with wide-eyed expectation. He took a big bite of his marmalade-covered croissant. "That should be fun."

He remembered, too late, he too hated marmalade.

But just for practice at concealing how he really felt, he chewed thoughtfully and proclaimed it delicious.

Sophie was looking at him as if she didn't believe him. What if she proved to be the person who could see right through all the masks he'd become so adept at wearing?

For some reason that thought was scarier than the four years he had just spent in a den full of rattlesnakes.

Because it threatened him as he had never once allowed himself to be threatened.

It went to the core he'd kept hidden.

What if Sophie Holtzheim could see his heart?

No worries, he tried to tell himself. He thought of the work he'd done. Four years building friendships. Building trust. He'd worked with those people, partied with them, attended the baptisms of their children and the marriages of the their daughters.

His work had culminated in twenty-three arrests in four

different countries. Bad guys, yes, but also people he had come to know on a different level: sons, husbands, fathers.

His own father probably knew the truth about him after all—Brand Sheridan's heart was as black as the ace of spades.

Early the next morning, Brand was working in his father's backyard, trying to clear the shambles his mother's rosebeds had become.

Nobody had to know that this is how he would honor her. Bring back something she had loved that now looked sorry and neglected. Who knew? Maybe with enough work it could be ready for next year's garden tour.

He was just blotting an angry, bleeding welt from a thorn when he got that hair-rising-on-the-back-of-his-neck feeling.

He turned slightly. The red hat was highly visible through the hedge. He smiled to himself. He was being watched.

"You must come see," Hilde called in German. "He's taken off his shirt."

He had taken off his shirt, even though the morning was cool, because the thorns were ripping it to tatters.

"Grandma!"

But out of the corner of his eye, he could see Sophie could not resist the temptation and had joined her grandmother at the hedge

He flexed a muscle for them, tried not to smile at the grandma's gasp of appreciation, pretended he had no idea they were there.

"He's bleeding," Hilde whispered, still in German. "You should bring him a Band-Aid."

"Stop it," Sophie said.

"Go over there," her grandma hissed.

"No."

"Ach. You have no idea how to conduct a romance."

"I do so. I was nearly married."

"Ha. Being flattered that someone pays attention to you is not the same as being romanced."

Brand knew it. Sophie hadn't been in love. She hadn't even been infatuated. She'd been *flattered.*

He picked up his shirt, wiped the sweat off with it, wandered over to the hedge, peered through it as if he was surprised to see them there.

"Hey, ladies, nice morning."

"Oh, Brand," Sophie said, and squeezed through the little gap in the hedge where she had made her escape the other night.

Or, from the annoyed glance back at the bobbing red hat, maybe she'd been pushed through it.

She was dressed for work. She looked as if she worked at a library, but he thought it was probably safe to assume the Historical Society would provide the same dusty-tomes atmosphere.

Her remarkable auburn hair had been pinned up, she was wearing a white shirt with a fine navy pinstripe, a stern, straight-line navy blue skirt and flat shoes.

She had her glasses on, making her reminiscent of the national-speech-contest girl she had once been.

Only now there was a twist.

Sophie was all grown up, and he was stunned to discover he harbored a librarian fantasy. It made his mouth go dry thinking of slipping those glasses off her face, pulling the pins from her hair, flicking open the top button of that primly fastened-to-the-throat blouse.

She intensified his commitment to the fantasy when she stared at him as if she was a sheltered little librarian, who had never seen a half-naked man before. She gulped, looked wildly back at the little hole in the hedge.

She brought out the sinner in him, because he was wickedly delighted in her discomfort. He folded his arms over his chest.

"You're bleeding," her grandmother coached, through the hedge, in German.

"You're, uh, very tanned," Sophie blurted out uncomfortably.

"I lived on a yacht in Spain."

"That was your undercover job?"

"Yes."

So many things she could have said: Was it glamorous? What's Spain like? Why a yacht? What was it like to live there? Were you pretending to be rich and famous? What did you do every day? Who were you trying to catch?

But she asked none of those.

She said, her eyes suddenly quiet on his face, "Were you afraid?"

Until this very moment, he hadn't thought so. But now, standing here in the quiet of the garden with her, the birds singing riotously in the trees, the odd bee buzzing by, he felt the complete absence of fear. And he felt a different kind of tension from the kind he had learned to live with, day in and day out, for four long years.

A delightful tension. A man aware of a woman. A woman aware of a man.

"I guess I was afraid," he admitted slowly. He wondered if he had ever said those words to another human being. It felt as though a vital piece of his armor fell away from him.

Not *It must have been exciting.* "It must have been unbelievably difficult."

He scrambled for the piece of fallen armor, grinned at her, flexed a muscle and was satisfied when her little tongue flicked out and gave the corner of her lip a nervous lick.

"Nah," he said, "just a job."

But despite the distraction, her eyes on his face were still quiet, *knowing*.

He hated that. "What happened to your engagement?" he asked, moving her away from the topic of *him*.

He hoped she wasn't going to tell him something that would make him have to hunt down her ex and have a little talk with him.

Sophie looked wildly uncomfortable.

"I should know," he encouraged her. "As your new beau, I should know why the last guy was dumb enough to ditch you."

"He didn't ditch me," she squeaked. "I told him I needed some time to think. While I was thinking, he was hunting. For my replacement."

Something in Brand whispered softly and entirely against his will, *as if you could replace a girl like her!* "What did you need to think about?"

Her eyes fastened on his naked bicep, he flexed it for her. She licked her lips.

"I don't know, exactly. *Something* was missing."

"Well, then you're a smart girl for calling it off."

"Do you really think so?"

"Really." Even he was surprised by how much he meant that. "You know, your parents were good, good people. They really loved each other, Sophie. Maybe you felt desperate to have what you had lost."

She looked stunned. He was a little shocked himself. Where had that observation come from?

"Ah, well," she said, looking away, finally, "I'm just

on my way to work, but I thought I should let you know I've formalized the plan."

She looked faintly relieved that there were actually neat papers in her hand, an escape from the intensity of the moment and the understanding that had just passed between them.

"I was just going to drop them in the mailbox, but since you're here—

Deliciously flustered, she thrust several sheets of neatly folded paper at him and ducked back through the hedge.

"You didn't say he was bleeding," her grandmother scolded in German. "A little first aid!"

"It wasn't life-threatening," Sophie said. "I'm late for work."

"I fear you are hopeless," her grandmother muttered.

He unfolded the sheets Sophie had handed him and sighed. He feared her grandmother might be right.

Under the boldface heading, **Courtship Itinerary**, Sophie had typed a neat schedule for their romance. It was obviously an effort to keep their arrangement all business, which a part of him applauded, though a different part became fiendishly more committed to shaking her safe librarian/historian world.

Tuesday: 7:00 p.m., bike to Maynard's, ice cream.
Friday: 7:30 p.m., movie at the old Tivoli.
Sunday: 3:00 p.m., swim at Blue Rock, weather permitting.

For a man who had taken weekend trips to Monte Carlo to gamble, attended yacht parties on unbelievably outfitted luxury craft, who had been wined and dined in some of the most famous restaurants in the world, her plan should have been laughable. This is what she had come up with for excitement?

This was the courtship of Miss Sophie?

But oddly, Brand didn't feel like laughing. He felt as if he was choking on something. The choices not made, a sweet way of life left behind.

He shuffled papers. The second sheet, also neatly typed and double-spaced, had the boldface title, **Courtship Guidelines**. As he scanned it, he realized it really meant Sophie's rules, starting with no public demonstrations of affection and ending with the request that he not call her Sweet Pea.

"Oh, lady," he said, crumpling up the rules, needing to regain his equilibrium, "you have so much to learn."

Or maybe he did. Maybe he was being given a chance to experience a choice not made a long time ago. Maybe it would be kind of fun to pretend to have the life he had walked away from.

Whistling, aware he felt inordinately happy despite the fact he was dancing with danger of a new kind—ah, well, danger had always held an irresistible pull for him—Brand worked a bit longer in the roses and then took the rose clippers to where the sweet peas were running riot along his father's back fence.

Though his mother had loved roses, Brand had always considered the sweet pea the loveliest flower she grew, in all its abundant and delicate pastel shades, the fragrance coming off those cheery blossoms like a little piece of heaven.

An overlooked flower, he thought, scorned by the serious gardeners who babied their roses and clipped their rhododendron bushes and pulled their dahlias in the fall.

Just like Sophie Holtzheim.

An overlooked flower.

When he'd clipped more sweet peas than he could hold in his arms, he went and filled the kitchen sink with water and dropped them in.

"What are you doing with my flowers?" his father asked grumpily, glancing up from his paper. His father apparently hadn't noticed there was nothing for breakfast in the house.

"I'm going to start a rumor," Brand said pleasantly. "And then I'm going to get some groceries. You want to come?"

"To start the rumor?" his father said hopefully.

"No, for the groceries. How come you don't have any food?"

"Why? You writing a report for your sister?"

"She's worried about you, Dad. You don't have to see her as the enemy. That fire rattled her."

"Rattled *her!* What do you think it did to me? Oh well, I didn't like cooking here anyway. Or eating here," Dr. Sheridan said, proud, reluctant. "It makes me miss your mother."

"I miss her, too, Dad. I come in this kitchen and think of strawberry lemonade and cookies warm from the oven, the chocolate chips dripping."

Something in his father's face softened, and, briefly, it almost felt that they might have a moment, share some fond memories. But his father rattled the paper and dove behind it.

Brand headed for the shower.

Later he went out to the bike shed, and found his mother's bike, complete with the basket which he filled with sweet peas until it overflowed. Then he rode right down Main Street, enjoying the pretense of being a small-town guy who had never, for the good of his country, done things that ate at his soul.

The thing that astonished him was how easy it was to slip from who he knew himself to be—a hardened warrior, heart of ice—into this role of a young man going to woo his girl.

Had he gotten that adept at playing roles?

At least this one had no grim, dark overtones. It just felt *fun*. It would be entertaining, fill up some of his time here, to play this game with Sophie. To break her rules, too.

Maybe, if nothing else, before he left here, he could teach Sophie to be spontaneous, though he doubted if he had enough time to tackle that particular challenge.

He parked the bicycle in front of the old two-story redbrick Edwardian building that housed the Historical Society, gathered the sweet peas in his arms, took the steps two at a time and stopped in front of the stern-faced woman at the reception desk in the outer office.

"I'm looking for my sweet pea," he announced, "Miss Sophie."

That would show Sophie Holtzheim just how sick and tired he was of other people making the rules that governed his life. He was on leave from his military duties. He wasn't taking orders from a little scrap of a girl!

Not unless they were the delicious kind. The librarian pulling her glasses off, chewing thoughtfully on the arm, watching him with heat in her eyes.

Brand Sheridan, he berated himself, *there is a special place in hell for guys like you.*

On second thought, he was already there.

The idea that this was going to be some kind of fun fled from him. He couldn't be sworn to help and protect Sophie and have these kinds of thoughts at the same time.

He needed to be a better man.

The courtship of Sophie was probably going to be the hardest assignment of his life.

CHAPTER FIVE

"YOU have a gentleman caller," Bitsy Martin whispered in the door of Sophie's office. "With flowers."

Sophie felt a blush rise up her cheeks. Of course, given how recently she had drawn up her rules of court-ship engagement, her gentleman caller could be only one person!

And of all the words she had ever used to describe Brand, and there had been many of them, most recently *pirate,* the word *gentleman* had never been on the list.

She didn't know which was more annoying: the fact that Brand had dispensed with her schedule, or the fact that Bitsy looked so amazed that a man would show up with flowers for her.

She didn't feel ready to deal with him. She still felt the stunning truth Brand Sheridan had so casually un-earthed this morning.

She had been going to marry Gregg Hamilton be-cause she missed her parents, had missed being part of that unit called a family.

Thank God he had not uncovered the whole truth. She was only just working toward that herself, and it was painful.

"I thought he was in the wrong place. He's what we would have called a rake back in the day," Bitsy confided. "Devilishly charming."

Again, there was something mildly insulting about Bitsy's disbelief that such a man would show up looking for *her*.

Sophie took a deep breath, got up and went down the hall. She tried to steel herself, but, of course, it was impossible.

The sweet-pea bouquet, abandoned on the counter, had already filled the entire office with its delicate fragrance. Brand had his back to her, restless, pacing, pretending to be interested in the old photos of Sugar Maple Grove that graced the walls.

Sophie fought the desire just to stop and drink in the sweeping masculine lines of that broad back, especially since Bitsy was watching.

Wait. That's the whole idea. To convince people we're actually interested in each other. Sophie could study the enticing lines of his back as long as she wanted. It was a heady freedom, as intoxicating as champagne, so she only allowed herself the tiniest sip before she cleared her throat.

"Brand," she said, her brightness forced, "An unexpected pleasure. What brings you here?"

She realized Bitsy was hovering with avid interest, and that for a girl who was supposed to be being romanced she sounded ridiculously formal. Her eyes skittered to the sweet peas. "My darling," she added as an afterthought. It sounded as if she had read a line from a script, badly.

He turned from the pictures on the wall and gazed at her, long and slow. He was going to be good at this! Way too good. Despite the fact that he said he had no girlfriends, she now suspected something else—dozens, *hundreds* of women wooed by the man with the perfect excuse to never commit!

He came back to the counter, leaned across it and planted a rather noisy—and distinctly demonstrative—kiss on her cheek.

"Ma chérie," he greeted her, his voice as liquid and sweet as warmed wild honey. It was as if he'd poured that honey over her naked body when he said something else in French, that she didn't understand but that was undoubtedly wicked.

"You don't speak French," she protested weakly to him.

"Actually, I do."

"I didn't know that." A French-speaking pirate. Whatever forces she had called down upon herself to test her sworn-off-love vow by burning pictures at midnight were extraordinarily powerful ones!

"There is quite a bit about me you don't know." How could he do that? That phrase was not *dirty*.

That was true. The boy next door had always been safe. Even in the darkest throes of her crush on him, there had never been the remotest chance of her love being requited. That had made it so safe somehow. Now, everything seemed different.

Especially him, something the same and something different meeting somewhere where she could not clearly see the lines, could not clearly discern the dangers.

"What did you say in French?"

"Just that I saw these flowers and they reminded me of you."

"Oh." Her cheek could not possibly be tingling! Sophie had to resist an impulse to reach up and touch her cheek where his lips had been.

"You want to go for lunch?"

"No!" Her voice sounded strangled.

He raised a wicked eyebrow at her, enjoying her discomfort, a pirate enjoying the game, enjoying his pretense of being a perfect gentleman.

"Of course you want to come for lunch with me," he coached her in a whisper, "you can't get enough of me."

Unfortunately, true.

"It's not lunchtime."

"That would not stop two people who were falling in love."

His eyes twinkled, a little grin tickled the sensuous curve of lips that had just touched her cheek. That she had tasted yesterday. That she wanted to taste again, with the desperate hunger of a woman who was falling hard and fast.

She'd always been way too susceptible to him. Always. It was time to claim her life back. Really. Past time.

Pull it together, girl, Sophie ordered herself. "Even if it is lunchtime, I couldn't possibly. Too busy." She heard Bitsy's muffled gasp of dismay, remembered they had a witness and that was what this was really all about.

It could only mean trouble that Sophie was aware of the growing disappointment that this was all an act, a role she had, very stupidly, encouraged him to play.

"What are you busy doing, Sweet Pea?" he asked, silkily, smooth, his eyes intent on her face, his fingers moving along the countertop, touching hers. He did a funny little thing with his fingertips, dancing them along her knuckles, feather-light, astonishingly intimate.

Instead of being pleased with his performance, Sophie wanted to cry. What had she gotten herself into? What woman wouldn't want a moment like this to be real?

His fingertips tickled her, drummed an intimate

little tattoo across the top of her hand, rested on the bone of her wrist.

Sophie's belly did that roller-coaster dive.

Unless she was mistaken, Bitsy gasped again, not with dismay but with recognition of something white-hot streaking through the stale air of the historical office—sexy, seductive.

"A box of memorabilia came in," Sophie stammered, and yanked her hand away. She brushed it across the top of her thigh, to make the tingling *stop*.

Brand's attention was on her hand, a faint smug smile of male knowing on a face that was just a little too sure of his ability to tempt, entice, seduce.

Unfortunately echoing what she had seen in Bitsy's face. Men like him didn't woo girls like her! Or use words like *woo* either, or as old-fashioned, as prissy, as archaic as *beau*.

Sophie had always been out of step. The sweet geek, walking dictionary, history buff, plagued by a certain awkward uncertainty in herself that she had managed to put away for ten minutes once to give a speech, but otherwise had never quite outgrown.

People didn't get why she had trouble getting over Gregg. No man had really ever noticed her before, and she despaired that one ever would again.

Except Brand.

He'd always noticed her. But in that aggravating, chuck-you-on-the-chin, you're-cute-and-funny-like-a-chimpanzee-who-can-ride-a-tricycle kind of way.

And Brand Sheridan? She had always noticed him, too, and not in the chimpanzee-on-a-trike kind of way.

He had always been hot. Not just good-looking, because really, good looks, while rare and certainly enticing, were not a measure of character. It wasn't even the fact that he had carried himself with such confidence, that he had radiated the mysterious male essence that stole breath as surely as bees stole nectar.

No, Brand had had a way of looking at people, and engaging with people that made them feel as if he could show them the secret to being intensely alive. There was something about him that had been bold and breathtaking.

In high school he had gone for the fast girls, Sophie remembered, a little more sadly than she would have liked. There had been a constant parade of them on the backseat of his motorcycle. Girls who were sophisticated and flirty, who knew how to wear makeup and how to dress in ways that men went gaga for.

She remembered she had tried to tell him once he was way too smart for that. That he should find a girl he could talk to.

What she had meant was a girl who was worthy of him. *Such as herself.*

If she recalled, he had thrown back his head and laughed at her advice, chucked her on the chin, said *Why do I need another girl to talk to, when I have you?*

Naturally, naive little fool that she had been, that off-the-cuff remark had sent her into infatuation overdrive.

He still thought she was that girl! And she was not doing one thing to set him straight!

It was stopping now. Sophie was not going to give him the satisfaction of being right! Even if he was!

Sophie pulled her hand away from her thigh and folded both her hands primly on the counter in front of her. She realized the gesture was a little too *old* for her.

It was time for a *new* Sophie to emerge, a woman who was not intimidated by the likes of him—or who could at least pull off the pretense that she wasn't!

She leaned forward and purred, "Beloved, as happy

as I am to see you, I must go back to work. I'm swamped. Simply swamped."

Out of all the endearments she could have picked, she kicked herself for choosing that one! Hopelessly dated. And fraught with emotion. *Beloved.*

To lean toward him and mean it. To let it be the last word on her lips at night and the first in the morning, to let it form in her mind when her eyes rested on him, even from a distance...

"Go away," she snapped at him, when he didn't seem to be getting it.

Another gasp from Bitsy. It was like working with her grandmother. Sophie turned and gave her a glare that she hoped would send her scuttling, but Bitsy stood her ground.

Feeling her hand was being forced, she leaned even closer, and tried to take the sting out of the "Go away."

"I'll make it up to you later." She blinked at him in her best version of the type of girl who had graced the back of his motorcycle.

A smile tickled those handsome lips. Unfortunately she couldn't tell if she'd managed to amuse him or intrigue him just the tiniest bit.

"I can help you with your work," he suggested, "and then we can go for lunch. Or we can go some place where you can make it up to me, whichever you prefer."

Done playing, Sophie picked up the sweet peas, opened the gate that separated the inner office from the outer one and let him through. She pointed down the hall and then marched behind him.

"That one," she said tersely.

He went into her open office, and she slid in behind him and then shut the door. With a snap.

She leaned against it trying to marshal herself.

There was no room for them both in her office, he had turned around to face her and was now leaning his rear up against her desk, arms folded over the solidness of his chest, eyes dancing with mischief and merriment.

At her expense.

His largeness made the room seem small and cramped. His vibrancy made the space—and her whole life—feel dull and dreary.

Her office was never going to feel the same now. Something of his larger-than-life presence was going to linger here and *ruin* it.

"What are you doing?" Sophie demanded.

He lifted a big shoulder, smiled. "Getting things started."

"We were supposed to start with a bike ride. To Maynard's. For ice cream. Tomorrow."

Every word sounded clipped, a woman in distress, a woman who had had a plan, and that plan included somehow needing a whole day to *prepare* to be with him.

"Ah, Sophie," he suggested, "lighten up. Be spontaneous."

"I don't like being spontaneous!" *Wait! Remember the new Sophie!*

"I seem to remember that," he said sympathetically, "Never too late to learn."

"I don't want to learn!" Which was a lie. The *new* Sophie thought spontaneity could begin with throwing herself at him and tasting his lips again.

That would wipe the smug look off his face!

"That's sad," he said.

"I am not sad! I will not have you see me as pathetic!" The urge to kiss him grew, just to prove something.

But it could backfire. It could prove she was even more pathetic than she thought.

"I don't see you as pathetic, Sophie, just...er...a little too rigid."

Rigid? This was turning into a nightmare. The world's most glorious man saw her as uptight and rigid? The *new* Sophie had to do something!

"Let's have some fun with this," he coaxed.

What could she say to that? She didn't like having fun? Now she felt driven to prove to him that she was not uptight and rigid!

That she could be flexible and fun.

And of course she could be.

Taking a deep breath, Sophie launched herself over the distance that separated them in a fashion that allowed no chickening out. She caught the widening of his eyes, his quick lean backward, but the desk prevented escape. She wrapped her arms around his neck and pulled him close.

She took his lips with hers.

There, she thought dreamily. That should show him. Nothing rigid or predictable about her. She could be spontaneous! She could have as much *fun* as the next person.

For a moment his lips softened under hers, and the word *fun* dissolved. Fun was a Fourth of July picnic or a new puppy or a good game of Scrabble.

This wasn't fun. It was intense. And dangerous. As exciting, as challenging as riding the rapids of an uncharted river or jumping from an airplane with a parachute that might or might not open.

This was part of her absolute gift for doing the wrong thing around him! She had set out to prove he didn't have any power over her anymore.

And proved the exact opposite. *Beloved.*

Not that he had to know. Ever.

That his lips tasted to her of everything she had longed

for when she had said yes to the wrong man and bought a wedding dress and collected pictures. Brand Sheridan's lips tasted of honey and dreams, of dewdrops and hope.

She had said to Gregg that she needed time to think, that *something* was missing.

Sophie reeled back from Brand, feeling aquiver with recognition. The rest of the truth she had been trying to hide from herself slammed into her.

The truth was she had nearly married Gregg because she had *never* wanted to feel love as deeply as she had felt it within her family again. She had wanted to have the security of that place called family, without the emotional investment that could devastate so totally. That could shatter a person's heart into a million jagged pieces. That could steal any semblance of remaining faith or hope from their soul.

Ultimately, Gregg had been safe. He would have never required her heart or her soul.

This man in front of her?

He would never be safe. And he would never accept less from the person he called *beloved* than their full heart, their complete soul.

Of course, with her gift for getting everything exactly wrong, here she was falling in love with the man least likely ever to call anyone *beloved*. The man who had made his work his built-in excuse for not loving anyone.

"There," she said, hoping she did not sound as shaken as she felt. "Spontaneity requirement met?"

"Not unless we were talking about spontaneous combustion," he muttered, his eyes as piercing as a pirate's on her face. Still, Sophie could tell she had managed to shock him.

What she couldn't tell was if it was in a good way. His eyes were unreadable, the mischief had gone from them.

She suddenly just wanted to hide.

If he had just followed the rules! If he had waited until tomorrow to go for ice cream instead of invading her world, he would have seen her at her most flexible. And fun.

She might have even managed flirty.

She might not have launched herself at him in a full-frontal attack! The sweet geek rides again! Gets it exactly wrong every time!

"Back to work," she said firmly. What she meant was back to her hidey-hole: words and dusty archives, glimpses into worlds long past that triggered her imagination, that she could immerse herself in when her own life seemed way too dreary, when the disappointment of the gap between what she desired and what she could have were inescapable.

She was not going to cry. "Nice of you to drop by. This box of stuff just came in," she fluttered a wrist at it, "and I need to go through it. It's time-consuming. All the letters have to be read—"

"This box?" he said, glancing at her, seeing what she did not want him to see if his faintly worried look was any indication.

Brand Sheridan was probably thinking she was more pathetic than he had ever guessed!

Still, intentionally or not—she suspected it was—he gave her a bit of space to compose herself.

He turned from her, opened the lid of the box, peered in. "I can read the letters for you. World War Two, right? I can sort through anything that pertains to that."

She could see him watching her quietly, waiting to see if she could accept his invitation to back up a bit, to get things back to normal.

How could it be normal after she had kissed him like

that? With his big assured self taking all the air out of her space? Applying all that confidence and curiosity to her stuff and her world?

Get him out of here, the old Sophie ordered her.

The new Sophie asked how could she have a drop of pride left if she let him see how damned rattled she was by the kiss she had instigated?

"Fine," she said, tightly. "We never turn down volunteer help. I understand you've been home in Sugar Maple Grove for nearly forty-eight hours. It's inevitable that the boredom is setting in. Let me set you up in the conference room."

She did. There. Now he could find out what boredom really was!

"Just keep out anything that pertains to the Second World War," she instructed him sweetly. "Bitsy can sort through the rest later."

And she closed the door firmly on him.

Brand found himself in the conference room, alone, the door shut on him. She'd done that deliberately, kissed him in retribution for his messing with her schedule, just to let him know what was going to happen if he messed with her—that she could be wild and unpredictable, too.

She couldn't really. She was as transparent as a sheet of glass. His sweet little next-door neighbor trying to be something she was not, trying to erase her image as a bookworm, wallflower, *librarian.*

She'd be surprised by how much Brand liked that about her. Sophie, with all her awkwardness and intellect, was different in a world where so much was same old, same old—cookie-cutter women who looked the same and talked the same and were the same.

Didn't Sophie know what a treat it was to unearth an

original? He smiled. A long time ago, before she was even old enough to know anything about anything, she'd shown disdain for his taste in women.

Still, for all that he knew she was trying to prove something to him that she couldn't, that kiss *had* been startling.

There had been something disturbingly wild and unpredictable in her lips meeting his for the second time.

What had he tasted?

Hunger.

More evidence that agreeing to romance Sophie had been about his worst idea ever.

Still, no wonder she'd fallen for the first guy to pay some attention to her. She wasn't just lonely for the family she had lost.

Nope, she was *hungry,* there was a fire in that girl only one thing was going to put out.

And it wasn't the fire that was roaring to life inside him just thinking about it. He hadn't come here planning to burn up with her. No, he'd wanted her to loosen up a little, throw out her rigidly uptight rule book, encourage her to be herself, to have a little unexpected fun.

The girl was like a tightly coiled spring of tension. Even her kiss had said that.

Ah, well, he'd sort through her dusty box for her, then take her out for lunch, coax that funny, lively original side of her to the surface.

With absolutely no kissing. He could be the better man. He could resist the temptation of Sophie…for her own good, of course.

He'd put out the fire he was feeling by giving his attention to the kind of stuff she did. If she'd been wrong that he was bored in Sugar Maple Grove—and she had been—the truth was that nobody was more surprised than him. He'd been here nearly two whole days and wasn't climbing the walls yet?

But the box she'd given him to sort through promised to change that!

Much as Brand appreciated that she had not been lured by the temptations of a glitzy world, he couldn't help but think, no wonder Sophie was so *ready* for a little excitement.

The box of so-called memorabilia contained things someone thought were important to the history of Sugar Maple Grove.

He forced himself to focus. He began to scan scraps of paper and old photos.

There were newspaper cuttings of the high-school basketball team making the state finals in 1972, faded color photos of the work team from Holy Trinity Church that had built an orphanage in Honduras in the eighties. There was a whitish-gray plaster mold of a hand that said Happy Mother's Day on the front, and on the back, in pen, Terry Wilson. Died Vietnam, 1969.

Brand had been dealing with subtle and not so subtle forms of evil for four years. For some reason, it felt as though this box immersed him in good, in the plain living of people with small-town values and humble ambitions.

To leave the world better.

No wonder Sophie had ended up here, at the Historical Society, documenting what made a small town tick.

There were several random items, including recipes and an old garter, possibly from a wedding.

And then, in the very bottom of the box, he found a packet of letters, tied up with a frayed black velvet ribbon.

Was this the gem of Second World War memorabilia he was supposed to be hunting for? Brand untied the ribbon, and plucked the first fragile letter out of the bundle. The envelope was addressed in a careful masculine hand to Miss Sarah Sorlington, General Delivery, Sugar Maple Grove. The return address was Private Sinclair Horsenell, a censor's heavy black pen blotting out the rest. But the postmark was February of 1942.

Pay dirt, he thought. Was this how Sophie got her thrills? It *was* kind of thrilling.

He carefully unfolded the letter from the young private. The paper was fragile along the fold marks, and the ink had begun to fade in places. Still, Brand was able to discern that Sinclair Horsenell had just disembarked in Ireland, part of the U.S. Army V Corps, the first Americans to deploy overseas.

"My dearest Sarah," he read, "what an extraordinary adventure I find myself on!"

The letter was beautifully descriptive of the lushness of Ireland, describing sights and sounds, camaraderie, funny incidents around the camp.

Despite all the new things I am seeing, and the grave sense of purpose I feel, the rightness of my being here, I miss you so deeply. I think of that last afternoon we spent and the picnic you prepared, the blue of your eyes matching the blue of the sky, and I feel both that I want to be with you, and that I want to be part of protecting the simple pleasures we were able to enjoy that afternoon. My darling, I am prepared to give my life for the protection of all that we hold dear.

I know you wanted to marry before I left, but that is not what I wanted for you. You deserve so much more than a rushed ceremony. I live to see you in a white dress, floating down the aisle toward me, a bouquet of forget-me-nots to match your eyes.

Wait for me, sweet Sarah. Wait.
Yours forever,
Sinclair

The letters had been carefully saved in their chronological order and Brand soon saw that Sinclair wrote faithfully, sometimes just a line or two, sometimes long letters. As the time passed, Brand noticed the excitement waning, giving way to the tedium of military life. Now the letters held occasional complaints about the lack of action, the officers, the terrible food.

The letter made Brand think, sadly, that things didn't change. Young men went away to war, and left sweethearts behind them.

"Did you find something?"

Things didn't change, but people did.

Sophie stood in the doorway, watching him, and he put away the letter he was reading.

Why did he feel reluctant to let her know what he had found? Because those letters were making him feel something. *Uneasy.*

"Just some old letters. They might have value. I haven't finished reading them yet. Bitsy is probably better qualified than me to decide what has historical value, but I'm willing to go out on a limb and guess these two items don't."

He handed her the recipe for Corn Flakes casserole and the garter.

She laughed, and it was a good sound. Not a girlish giggle, but genuine. He was unaware how he had longed for genuine things until he heard it. It pulled him toward her like a beacon guiding a fisherman lost in a fog.

"Are you ready for lunch?" she asked.

There was something shy in that, his old Sophie, not

the girl she had tried to convince him she was when she had kissed him. This Sophie's laughter was so genuine it made him ache.

Brand glanced at his watch, amazed at how much time had gone by. Somehow the genuineness in her, coupled with the genuineness of the emotion in Sinclair's letters made him feel bad about playing with Sophie's world.

He didn't want to have lunch with her and look at her lips and be the kind of guy who plotted another taste of them.

"You know what?" he said. "You were probably right. Let's follow your schedule. I'll see you tomorrow night after supper. We'll ride our bikes down Main Street, go for ice cream. It will be a highly visible activity that the whole town can see."

She stared at him. Disappointed? Annoyed?

That was good, he tried to tell himself. If they were going to carry off this *courtship* thing with no one getting hurt, it would be for the best if she found him disappointing and annoying.

"I'll take these with me," he said, gathering up the letters. "And get them back to you when I'm finished going through them."

Why did he feel that he had to protect her from the letters? They were just sweet letters a young, heartsick man had written home.

For some reason, Brand wanted to make sure they had a happy ending.

As though he needed to protect her if they didn't.

He had a feeling this desire to protect Sophie was going to do nothing but get him in trouble. Especially since it was now evident this was a more complicated mission than he had first perceived.

He had to protect her from himself and his reaction to her *hunger.*

"See you tomorrow," he said breezily. "Are you still a purely vanilla girl?"

"You think I'm really boring," she said.

Her lips had already told him there was a secret side to her that was anything but boring, but he was determined he wasn't going there.

He thought of the world he had lived in for four years, where God forbid anybody should ever be bored, and so they had become adept at manufacturing all the excitement money could buy. And become so addicted to it, they were prepared to do anything to keep a lifestyle they had not legitimately earned, were not legitimately entitled to.

He thought of the letters in his hand, letters from a young man who was probably beginning to yearn for all those things he had once called boring.

"Don't," he told Sophie sternly, moving by her, the letters in his hand, "say *boring* as if it's a bad thing."

CHAPTER SIX

SOPHIE could not resist going to the window and watching Brand get on an old bicycle and peddle away. It was a woman's bike, and ancient. Probably it had belonged to his mother.

And yet, the way he rode it, he could have been a knight and the bike a war horse. With his colossal confidence he could probably stride down Main Street in a pair of canvas pirate's pants, and nothing else without flinching.

Not that she wanted to be thinking about him like that! Why would he flinch? She had seen his considerable assets, seen him without his shirt, the perfection of skin stretched taut over hard muscle marred only by recent thorn scratches. He knew what he had, the devil, and probably knew exactly the effect it had on women!

The man was maddening! He'd tempted her to kiss him! He had *made* her feel driven to show him that just because she was a small-town girl, naive and heartbroken, his big strong self was not going to march into her world and take control of everything!

Ha! She was going to show him. That kiss had just been a start!

Though when she thought of that it occurred to her

she wasn't quite ready to mess with a force that had the potential for so much power.

Even thinking about that, her hand moved to her lips, to the puffiness where his lips had touched her lips— collided really—and she felt a shiver, of longing, of awareness, of aliveness.

No, she had better stick to surprising him with small things.

"Vanilla ice cream, indeed. Tiger passion fruit," she told herself. "Or banana fudge chunk."

That's it, girl, she added silently, *live dangerously.*

But she already knew that once you had played with the danger of lips like his, the chances of erasing the thrill of that memory were probably slight to nil.

Sophie willed herself to be only annoyed with Brand for messing with her plans, for tilting her tidy world so off-kilter, for making her want so badly to be seen in ways she had never been seen before.

And probably never will be, she thought with a resigned sigh.

He was a force to be reckoned with, fast and furious, like a hurricane sweeping through. Only a fool thought they could play with a hurricane, or tame it or force it onto a path other than the one it had chosen.

But the scent of the sweet peas filled her office, a poignancy in the fragrance that made it hard to be annoyed, and harder still to build her defenses against his particular kind of storm. It reminded her everything was more complicated than that.

He wasn't just a hurricane.

Sometimes, like when he'd leaned across that counter this morning and played with her fingertips, he was so much what she had remembered him being a devil-may-care boy, full of himself and mischief, his charm abundant, his confidence reckless.

But when she had walked into that conference room and he had looked up at her, and refused to go for the lunch he'd invited her on, it had not been that boy.

Or a hurricane, either.

It had not even been the man she had stolen a daring kiss from.

That new veil had been down in Brand's eyes, something remote and untouchable, the fierce discipline of a warrior surrounding him like impenetrable armor.

That had never been in him before. Something hard and cold, a formidable mountain that defied being climbed. It was something lonelier than the wind howling down an empty mountain valley on a stormy winter day.

She shivered thinking about it, and thinking about the kind of bravery it would take to tackle what she had seen in his eyes, to ignore the No Trespassing signs, to try and rescue him from a place he had been and could not leave.

Sophie, she scoffed at herself, *you don't know that.*

But the problem was that she did. And now that she knew it, how could she walk away and leave him there?

Even if that's what he thought he wanted?

The next evening Sophie dressed carefully for their outing to the ice-cream parlor. Her war with herself was evident in her choices: her shorts rolled a touch higher up her thigh than they would normally have been, the V in her newly purchased halter top a touch lower.

Just in case that kiss had not done the trick, she was not going to be dismissed as the little sweet geek from next door! She wanted the days of Brand Sheridan feeling like her brotherly protector to be over!

And at the same time, she didn't want him to get the

idea she was trying to be sexy *for him*, because she thought probably every girl in the world had tried way too hard around him for way too long.

So she wore no makeup and pulled her hair back into a no-nonsense ponytail.

Her grandmother approved of the outfit, but not ice cream or bike-riding as romantic choices.

"He loves ice cream, Grandma, he always has."

"Ach. Do you have to ride your bike to get it? You'll be all sweaty. And your hair!" She was still squawking away in German when she went to answer the door.

In German: "The hair! It makes you look like a woman I used to buy fish from." In English, "Hello, Brand," in German, "She died lonely."

"It could have been the fish smell," Sophie said, in English, because it was too complicated to figure out how to say it in German. Did her hair look that bad? Not just the careless do of a woman confident in herself?

Brand stepped in, and Sophie was anxious about who had come: the carefree boy from next door, or the new Brand, the weary warrior.

It was the warrior, something in him untouchable. The smile that graced his lips did not even begin to reach his eyes.

Just like that, it wasn't about her. It was not, she thought, pulling the band from her hair, a good thing to die lonely.

"Everything okay?" she asked him quietly, as she gathered her bag and slipped out the door he held open for her. She glanced at his face.

He looked startled, as if he had expected the smile to fool her. "Yeah, fine."

She looked at him, again, longer. It wasn't. So, she would work from the present, backwards until she found out what had put that look on his face.

And then what? she asked herself, and when no answer came she hoped she would just know when the time came.

"How are things with your dad?" she asked, casually, as they went down the steps. She thought something had happened in the conference room, but the rejection of his father couldn't be helping.

"Why don't you tell me? How are things with my dad? Is he okay in that house by himself?"

She was aware he was trying to divert her, as if he had sensed she was going to try and go places angels feared to tread.

"Your dad is one of the most capable men I know."

"That answers your question then, doesn't it? Things with my dad are fine."

He got astride the old girl's bike, waited for her...she didn't miss the fact that he looked long and hard at her legs and then took a deep breath and looked away.

"Except for the little matter of him catching his house on fire," he muttered, as they began to pedal down the quiet street, side by side. "Why don't you tell me what you know about that?"

Somehow he had turned it around! He was being the inquisitor. And she'd bet he was darn good at it, too, when he put that cold, hard cop look on his face.

"I'm not spying on your dad for you!"

"You know what happened," he said, watching her face way too closely.

Well, yes, she did. But Dr. Sheridan had specifically asked her not to tell Brand that he and her grandmother had been caught in a fairly compromising position as the house burned around them. He had also asked her, last night, just before he had taken Hilde for dinner, not to mention that he and her grandmother were having a *real* romance.

"But don't you think he'll notice?" Sophie had asked, uncomfortable to be put in yet another position of deception.

"I'm counting on you to be a distraction," the doctor had said pleasantly.

"But why don't you just tell him?"

"He'll see it as a betrayal of his mother. Brand is a man who *likes* being lonely."

Now, looking at the coolly removed expression on Brand's face, Sophie could see there was some truth in the doctor's assessment of his son. Brand had developed a gift for distance.

Who was this man? Once he would have tried to argue it out of her, tease it out of her, coax it out of her.

Now he just cast her a look that was coolly assessing, said nothing more about the fire and quickened his pace so that his bike shot ahead of hers.

And, as aggravating as she had found his appearance in her office yesterday, as much as she had felt vulnerable to him, Sophie decided to try another tack to coax that chilly look off his face and bring the boy she had always known back to the surface.

Sophie put on a bit of steam herself, pulled out beside him and then passed him. She took the lead, then turned around, placed her thumb on her nose and waggled her fingers at him.

"Ha, ha," she said, "you have a girl's bike!"

So much for the new Sophie, all slick sophistication and suave polish.

Brand had always been competitive, and he read it as the challenge she had intended. Just as she had known, he could not resist. She could hear the whir of his bike spokes, the rubber tires hissing on the pavement. She pedaled harder. She was on an eighteen-speed, he on a three. He was going to have to work very hard to keep up with her.

Apparently he was up to the task. When she heard him coming up on her right-hand side, she swerved in front of him, heard his yelp of surprise as she cut him off and kept the lead.

"Hey," he called, "you're playing dirty!"

Her laugh of fiendish enjoyment was entirely genuine. She rose off the seat, leaned forward, stood up on those pedals and went hard.

Mr. Machalay crept out on the road in front of her, one arm full of groceries, the other clamped down on the leash of his ancient dog, Max. She rang her bell frantically and swerved around them. She glanced over her shoulder. Brand swerved the other way around Mr. Machalay and Max, both of whom now stood frozen to the spot. Mr. Machalay dropped the leash and waved his fist at them.

"Sorry," she called. Still, she was pleased with her lead. It didn't last long.

"You're going to cause an accident," he panted, way too close to her ear.

"Oh, well," she called back, breathless. "Better than dying of boredom."

"I thought I told you that wasn't a bad thing!"

"Coming from the great adventurer, Brand Sheridan, I found that a little hard to buy."

"Watch your tone," he instructed her, exasperated. "You're supposed to adore me!"

She laughed recklessly.

"You needn't make that sound as if it's impossible," he called, and then he pulled his bike up right beside her.

Sophie thought she'd been pedaling with everything she had, but a sudden whoosh of adrenaline filled her and she dug deep and found something extra.

They were racing full-out, and she loved the breathless feeling, loved the wind in her hair, her heart pumping, her muscles straining. She loved knowing he was beside her. She felt as if she had been asleep and suddenly she was gloriously, wonderfully alive.

He reached out over the tiny distance between them, and touched her, a gentle slap on her shoulder, as if they were playing tag, and then he surged ahead, effortlessly, as if he had only been playing with her all along.

Though his bike was older and less sound, his legs were longer and stronger. But it was his heart, the fierce, competitive heart of a warrior, that made this race impossible for her to win.

She cast him a look as he shot by and smiled to herself. She might not win this race, but she had won in another way.

It was there. A light shone in his face, laughter sparked in his eyes, the line of his mouth, though determined, had softened with fun. It took her back over the years and made her think maybe she did not have to go as far as she thought to find him where he was lost.

Now he was way out in front, weaving fearlessly in and out of the growing traffic as they got closer to Main Street and downtown.

He turned, put his thumb to his nose, waggled his fingers at her as she had done to him. "I might have a girl's bike, but I'm no girl!"

"Don't say that as if there's something wrong with being a girl!"

And then they were both laughing, and he deliberately slowed up and let her catch him.

"Nothing at all wrong with being a girl," he told her, sweetly, solemnly.

By the time they arrived at Maynard's they were

together, the couple that they hoped to convince everyone they were.

He threw down his bike, and lay on the grassy boulevard, taking deep breaths, looking up through the canopy of leaves to the sky.

She threw down her own bike, and saw he was choking on laughter. It was a good sight and a good sound. She had broken down the barrier around him, and she was satisfied with that.

She lay down on the grass beside him. Who cared who saw them? Wasn't that the point? Thanks to Grandma she kept her arms glued to her sides in case she was sweaty.

"You nearly killed me," he accused her.

"That would be a cruel irony, wouldn't it? With all the things you've seen and done, to die racing your bicycle down the Main Street of Sugar Maple Grove?"

The laughter was gone.

"Yeah," he said, "that would be a cruel irony."

"What have you seen and done?" she whispered, seeing his defenses down, moving in. *Tell me.*

But he got up and held out his hand to her, pulled her to her feet. She hoped any sweat had dried, but if there was any, he didn't notice or didn't care.

He stood staring at her for a long time, debating something.

She held her breath, knowing somehow he needed this.

And yet not at all surprised when he was able to deny his own need.

Instead, he kidded, "What have I seen and done? Ice-cream flavors you wouldn't believe."

"Such as?"

"On the tame side, Philippine mango. On the wild side, ox tongue in Japan."

"Ox-tongue ice cream?" she said skeptically.

"Or oyster, garlic, or whale. Seriously."

"Did you try those?"

"Of course. Who could resist trying them?"

At the risk of confirming she was boring, she stated, "Me!"

"You only live once. Rose petal is a favorite in the Middle East. You might like that."

"You've eaten rose-petal ice cream?"

"Yeah."

"Really?"

"Really."

And the moment when he had almost told her something, revealed a hidden part of himself was gone, but this was something, too, to have him relaxed at her side, remembering exotic flavors of ice cream, and unless she was mistaken, *enjoying* this little slice of small-town life.

"Surprise me," he told her. "Order something other than vanilla."

And then Sophie was duty-bound to order vanilla, since he had suggested something else!

"Not unless they have rose petal," she decided. "Or if they have ox tongue I might try that."

And he laughed, because they both knew she never would, not even if she was starving to death and ox-tongue ice cream was the only food left on the face of the earth.

After they had gotten their ice cream in chocolate-dipped waffle cones, they left their bikes lying on the grassy boulevard, unlocked, and strolled down Main Street. The evening was not cooling, and even as light leached from the sky it was so hot that the ice cream was melting faster than they could eat it.

There was something about this experience: walking down Main Street with him, licking ice cream while the sun went down on a day that had been scorching hot, that was both simple and profound. She didn't know what it said about her life that this felt like one of the best moments ever.

And it didn't hurt that other women were looking at her with unabashed envy, either! Or that he seemed oblivious to the fuss he caused, to the sidelong looks, to the inviting smiles, as if being with her was all that mattered.

Was he really that good an actor? No, he'd always had that gift. No matter who he had been with, it had always felt as if, when he focused on her, she was all that mattered to him.

He stopped in front of an art gallery, closed for the day.

"Like any of them?" he asked her of the paintings in the window. He crunched down the last of his cone, and licked some stray ice cream off the inside of his wrist.

It was so sexy she nearly fainted.

She studied the paintings with more intensity. "I like that one," she decided, finally. It was safe to glance at him. No more ice-cream licking. "The one with the old red boat tied at the end of the dock."

"What do you like about it?"

It took my mind off what you could do with that tongue if you set your mind to it. And she bet he had set his mind to it. Lots.

"The promise," she stammered. "Long summer days that just unfold without a plan."

Moments caught in time, she thought, moments like this one that somehow became profound without even trying.

"Somehow I have trouble imaging you without a plan," he said.

"I'm not uptight!" *Though a woman whose mind went in twisted directions over a lick of ice cream was probably, at the very least, repressed.*

"Of course you aren't," he said soothingly, smiling at her in an annoying way, as if he was going to pat her on the head. Then he studied the painting.

"It's been a long time since I spent a day like that," he said, and something slipped by his guard. Wistfulness?

"You were never the type of guy who did things like that," she reminded him. "A day fishing? Too quiet for you."

"I know, I was the guy roaring down Main Street on my secondhand motorcycle with no muffler. Leaping from the cliff *above* Blue Rock, that outcrop that we called the Widow Maker. Jumping my bicycle over dirt-pile ramps at high speeds."

"Which you have just proven you still are!"

He smiled, but the wistfulness was there. "After I wrecked my third bicycle my dad wouldn't buy me another one. Everything seemed simple back then," he said. With a certain longing?

Could she help him back to that? And also prove she could be spontaneous, not uptight? A girl who could surrender her plan?

"Want to try it?" she asked. "I could find a boat. Your dad has fishing rods. We could dig some worms."

The new Sophie was appalled, of course, and her grandmother would be, too. What kind of romance plan was that? Digging worms? But the truth was she was suddenly way more anxious to see him enjoy himself, truly and deeply, than she was to manipulate his impressions of her.

Except for the impression that she had to have a plan.

"It's not on the courtship list," he teased her.

"I can adjust the list."

He shrugged, amused. "You can?" he asked, with faked incredulousness. "It's your courtship, Sophie. If you want to dig worms and go fishing, I'll go along."

Good. He'd be so much more amenable if he thought this was about her and not him.

"We can go tomorrow after work," she decided. "I'll track down a boat. Can you look after the worms?"

"Sorry, I'm not depriving you of the pure romance of digging worms with me."

And then he was laughing at the look on her face, and that laughter was worth any price. Even digging worms!

Sophie was less certain when she stood beside him the next evening in his mother's rose garden.

"This looks good," she said of the rose garden, amazed at how the weed-choked beds and overgrown roses were beginning to look as good as they once had. "You've done a lot in a little amount of time."

He handed her a jar with some dirt in it. "Enough small talk. Dig. Worms. Big ones. Wriggly ones. Juicy ones. Ones just like this!"

He dangled a worm in front of her face.

She screamed, and he chuckled. "Come on, Sweet Pea, you were never the kind of girl who was scared of creepy-crawly things."

"I was. I just pretended not to be."

"Really? Why?" He took the jar from her, dropped the worm into it without making her touch it.

"If I had let those boys know I had a weak spot, Brand, I would have been finding worms in my lunchbox, worms in my books and worms in my mittens."

"There was a certain group of boys who picked on

you," he recalled affectionately. "Especially after 'What Makes a Small Town Tick.'"

"I think they might have made my life unbearable except for the fact they knew my big, tough next-door neighbor had my back. Brand Sheridan. My hero." She slid him a little look. He was on his hands and knees filling the worm jar, not even asking her to help.

"Actually, I think they probably liked you. You know, guys at a certain age give the girl they like a frog, so she won't know, and so they can hear her scream. I probably prevented you from having a boyfriend for a lot of years when you could have. Or should have."

"I felt like you had my back then," she said, her voice soft with memory, "and here we are, eight years later. And you still have my back."

He glanced up at her, smiled, looked back and snagged a wriggler from the freshly turned black soil and put it in his jar. "I'll always have your back, Sophie."

He said that so casually, but even the casualness of the statement resonated deeply with her, and made her heart stand still. The way he said it, it was as if caring about her was part of who he was, came as naturally to him as breathing.

Just as she was relaxing, he turned and tossed a worm at her and then laughed when she shrieked. A good reminder that for all his sterling qualities, Brand Sheridan was no saint!

"Are you trying to tell me you like me?" she demanded.

"Sure. That, and I wanted to hear you scream. Did those boys stop bugging you by high school, Sweet Pea?"

"By then they ignored me completely," she admitted. "I was the invisible girl."

And somehow, even though this fishing trip was

supposed to be all about him, it was so easy to tell him about her. To talk about the lonely little geek she had once been, not with regret, but with affection.

And it became so easy to show him the life he had said such a firm "no" to eight years ago.

They went fishing at Glover's Pond, but before they got there they had to go through the ritual of him chasing her around the garden with his jar of worms. And then they had to go to Bitsy's house and load her long-dead husband's old wooden rowboat onto the roof of Brand's car—a sporty little number which was not made to carry old wooden rowboats.

After much cursing and sweating and laughing and yelling of orders, they finally made it out of Bitsy's driveway.

And when they got to the pond they had to reverse getting that contraption on the roof, to get it back off.

"Get out of the way," Brand panted at her, trying single-handedly to wrestle the rowboat off the roof of his car. "I don't want you squished by a damn boat."

"Shut up. You're such a chauvinist."

"Get out of the way!"

"Okay. Okay."

"Was that sound my paint job getting scratched?" His voice from underneath the rowboat was muffled.

"You wanted to do it by yourself, Mr. Macho! Now you have a scratch. Live with it."

"Mr. Macho. Are you kidding me? Who says things like that?" he muttered, wobbling his way down to the water with the rowboat on top of him. "How bad's the scratch?"

"Small. About the same size as the worm you threw at me. Maybe worms make good Bondo. Have you ever thought of that?"

"Actually, no, I never have. Imagine that."

He flipped the boat off, kicked off his shoes and hauled it into the water without rolling up his pants. The boat didn't start to float until he was in nearly to his thighs.

"That painting, Sweet Pea? A big, fat lie! Don't get wet, for God's sake. One of us getting wet is enough."

He shoved the boat around, waded back in, guiding it with a rope attached to the pointed bow. Then he stooped, moved his shoulder into her stomach, wrapped his arms around her knees and lifted. She found herself being carried like a sack of potatoes out to the boat. He lowered her in.

When the excitement of being manhandled by him, and having an intimate encounter with his shoulder subsided, she couldn't help but notice her feet were getting wet. Already.

"Brand?"

"What?"

"The boat appears to be leaking."

He peered in over the side. "It's not like a leak. It's a dribble. That's what the coffee can is for."

And then he nearly dumped the boat trying to scramble over the side to get in. Finally in and settled, he attached the oars while she bailed water from around their ankles. No matter how fast she bailed, the water level stayed about the same.

"Are you sure its just a dribble?"

"Hey, I'm a marine. If the boat goes down, I'll save you."

If that was anything like being manhandled by him, she'd better bail harder.

After a while, he set the fishing lines and handed her a pole, while he bailed and rowed. And swatted bugs.

"I've got a nibble," she cried, rising unsteadily to her feet.

"No, you don't. Sweet Pea. Sit down. You can't stand up in boats. Sit down!"

He was quite masterful when he used that tone of voice. She sat down.

"I lost the fish," she told him.

"I'm beginning to think fishing is overrated, anyway." He rowed them in a big circle around the pond.

It was a ridiculous way to conduct a courtship, Sophie thought. No flowers, no wine, no fancy dinner, no dancing until dawn. But she was the one who never seemed to get anything right.

But if that was true, why did this feel so right? Probably because watching him pit his strength against a water-filled boat that was growing more uncooperative by the second was just about as sexy as watching him lick ice cream off his wrist.

"You know that painting?" he asked her.

"Uh-huh."

"There's a reason no one's in the damn boat."

And then they were laughing, and the sun was going down, and the water sloshing around her ankles felt wonderful, though not as wonderful as watching him pit his pure strength against the oars until it was so dark they could hardly see each other anymore.

As they exited the boat and wrestled it back up the slippery bank toward his vehicle, the evening seemed to be ringed with magic, suffused with a golden light.

"I'm picking the next date," he told her, swatting at a mosquito. "If this was your idea of romantic, you are in big trouble."

"It may not have been romantic," she said, "but it was fun, and Brand, given a choice, I think I'd choose fun."

He rolled his eyes. "Fun over romance. Good grief, girl, what kind of a dork were you engaged to, anyway?"

"Don't even pretend you know what a dork is," she teased him.

"But I do, Sweet Pea. Because you taught me."

"So, what is your idea of a romantic date?" she asked him.

"Given the limited choices of the town, its probably still the movies on Friday night."

"This week's feature is *Terror in the Tunnel*. Even you can't make that romantic."

"That just goes to show what you know. It's not about the movie. Besides, if we're trying to be highly visible, I don't think Glover's Pond quite does it."

Sophie decided that Brand Sheridan was both the easiest man she had ever spent time with and the hardest. It was so easy to talk to him, to be with him, to laugh with him, and so hard when she remembered the truth: this was all a charade.

As she was getting ready to go to the movie, it felt *real*. The hammering of her heart, the tingling anticipation she felt waiting for the doorbell to ring, the way her heart swooped when she saw him in the door watching her come toward him. It felt all too real.

Especially the palpable electrical tension between them.

"Showtime," he said, parking as close to the theater as he could and holding open her door for her. "Pretend you love me, Sweet Pea."

He paid for the show, Sophie slipped out her wallet to pay for the popcorn.

He gave her a look. "Not even in a pretend world would I ever let that happen," he growled in her ear.

The theater was packed. Before the movie started, everyone was sending surprised looks their way. Several people were nudged by others, turned in their seats and craned their necks to look at Sophie and her new beau.

"You were right about this date," she whispered to him, "highly visible."

The lights went down. The movie started. With a bang. A terrible explosion filled the screen.

Sophie gasped. She *hated* this kind of movie.

And then his hand found hers in the darkness.

"I'm okay," she whispered. "It just startled me." When he didn't let go of her hand, she leaned closer to him, "You don't have to do that. No one can see us."

"When we walk out of here, it will be written all over you that we did this."

"It won't!"

"If it's done right, it will."

"You are just a little too sure of yourself, mister," she hissed.

"I know," he growled in her ear, "but my supreme confidence in myself is not unfounded."

And then he did that thing with his fingertips on her knuckles, even though that was not in the rules, even though no one could possibly see them. Just when she thought maybe, *maybe,* she could get accustomed to the pure masculine possessiveness of his touch without her heart doing double-time, he moved his hand up to her wrist and traced slow, sensuous circles around the delicacy of her bones.

Who knew wrists could be such zones of sensation?

When he had thoroughly debilitated her with the wrist thing, he turned her hand over, and his fingers did the same sensuous exploration on the palm of her hand.

Throughout the movie he toyed with her fingers. He lifted her hand to his lips and kissed it, he treated her wrist and her palm as if they were parts of the female body that were worshipped in one of those exotic places he had been.

When the final credits rolled, she didn't know what the movie had been about and she could barely get out of her seat. She stumbled so badly in the aisle that he wrapped his arm around her waist and pulled her in close to him.

"I tried to warn you," he whispered.

"Warn me about what?" she said proudly.

"That it would be written all over you."

"It's not."

He gazed at her, smiled wickedly, "Oh, yeah, baby, it is."

"It isn't."

"Okay, smarty, what was the movie about?" Before she could gather her wits to answer, they had passed through the lobby and were on the street.

"Oh, oh," he said, "heads up, Sophie, it's showtime. For real."

What did that mean? What had happened in there wasn't real? Then she saw Gregg coming toward them, Antoinette in tow.

Suddenly she felt glad that all those moves Brand had done with his hands *showed*.

Antoinette, naturally, was gorgeous—tall, raven-haired, blue-eyed. "Sophie," Gregg said. "And it was Brandon, wasn't it? I want you to meet my Toni."

Sophie thought this rated very high on the awkward-moment list, but naturally Toni was way too classy to let that show.

"You're the woman I owe the biggest thank-you to!" she said. "I'd been watching this guy from the back row of a law class for two years. Oh, my God, when I heard he was available, I pounced. Poor guy didn't know what hit him, did you, sweetie?"

Gregg looked flustered, thrilled and in love.

"And how long have you two been seeing each other?" Antoinette asked.

"Forever," Sophie blurted out at the same time as Brand said, "Just a little while."

Sophie laughed nervously. She should have never uttered that word *forever* in reference to him. Not even as part of the charade, because it opened up a yawning hole of yearning in her that nothing was ever going to be able to fill.

Brand tucked her closer into him. "We've known each other forever," he covered for her.

"Oh," Antoinette said, contemplating them with the genuine interest of someone who liked everyone, "Is it serious?"

"No," Sophie said.

"Yes," Brand said.

Antoinette laughed. "Careful, Sophie, he has that look of a man who gets what he wants. Are you two going to Maynard's? Gregg tells me everyone goes after the show. It's so charming and small-town. I can't wait."

"No," Sophie said. "We're not going."

At the very same time, Brand said, "Of course we're going. *Everyone* does."

"See you there, then. Ta-ra." Antoinette wagged her fingers at them, tucked her arm into Gregg's and they disappeared into the thinning after-show crowd.

Sophie was silent as Brand opened the car door for her. She slid in, waited until he started the car.

"I don't want to go to Maynard's."

"Relax. It's a test. You're going to pass."

But the test felt as if it had changed, and she wasn't going to pass if he did that thing to her wrist again!

She let him think she didn't want to go because of

Gregg and Antoinette. "She represents an unfair distribution of attributes," she decided sulkily. "She's smart and she's beautiful. Did she have to be nice, too?"

Brand said nothing.

After a while, she asked, "Did *you* think she was beautiful?"

"Sure. And smart. And nice."

"Oh."

"Sophie, her being those things doesn't make you any less than."

"She's the one he threw me over for!"

"Technically, you let him go."

"Well, I was going to take him back, after I did some thinking."

"So, she's smart, she's beautiful, she's nice *and* she prevented you from making the biggest mistake of your life. I'm liking her more by the second."

Suddenly, the situation they were heading into didn't feel awkward. It felt good, as if maybe Sophie could trust things to work out the way they were supposed to, even if it wasn't the way she had envisaged.

"Thanks, Brand," she said.

"Don't thank me too soon," he said. "I'm not done with you yet. By the time we walk out of Maynard's the whole town is going to know you are so over him."

"What are you planning?

"Just a little romance."

"You're scaring me."

"In my world, a little fear is never a bad thing." He pulled up in front of Maynard's and took her hand as they walked in. As they stepped over the threshold, he pulled her hand up to his lips and lightly kissed where their fingers were intertwined.

After that, she walked to the table in a daze. As they

settled into their seats, he let go of her hand, but with seeming reluctance.

"Ever come here with him after the movie?" he asked. The waitress came and offered them menus. Sophie took one, but he shook his head. "I know what I want," he said, not taking his eyes off Sophie.

The waitress stared at him, looked at Sophie and sighed, "You lucky girl."

"That's how you let the whole town know you're so over him," Brand said with satisfaction when the waitress left, promising to come back in a minute for their order.

"You're embarrassing me," Sophie managed to choke.

"Excellent. You blush when you're embarrassed. Naturally, it will be mistaken for the throes of love."

Mistaken? Dear God, this was feeling less like a charade every minute. She was going to be in deep trouble if Brand kept this up.

"So did you come here with the ex?"

Sophie nodded.

"So, what did you do?"

"Ordered hot chocolate. Drank it. Went home."

"What did you do that was *romantic?*"

She was sure she must have done something, but Brand kissing on her fingers, looking at her with such white-hot intensity and saying he *knew* what he wanted, seemed to have addled her mind, because not one thing she had ever done could compare to this.

When she didn't answer, Brand regarded her sympathetically. "What did he do that was romantic?"

She had to think very hard.

"He held out my chair for me."

"Did he hold your hand?"

"We were drinking hot chocolate!"

Brand looked unimpressed. "Gaze into your eyes? Reach across and fiddle with your hair? Play with your feet under the table?"

His foot reached out and caressed her calf. He grinned evilly before he pulled it away. She felt as if her face was on fire.

"Perfect," he purred.

Antoinette and Gregg came in just then, and Brand watched them unabashedly. Gregg pulled out Antoinette's seat, then turned and talked to the people at the table behind him.

"Anything you did with him" Brand said, turning back to her with a shake of his head, "do the opposite with me."

"I don't know what that means." If he reached out and fiddled with her hair, she'd probably faint and slide under the table like someone who had drunk too much champagne. That was the effect he had on her.

"Okay. Just follow my lead."

The waitress came back. "Sophie, you want something off the menu or your usual?"

"My usual. Hot chocolate."

Brand made an exasperated sound deep in his throat. "The opposite," he reminded her in an undertone. When she didn't get it, he sighed.

"Cancel the hot chocolate. We'll have one large fudge sundae. Don't skimp on the whipped cream and don't forget the cherry."

"Two spoons?" the waitress asked.

"Yes," Sophie said, feeling control slipping away from her as quickly as a glass covered in cooking oil.

"No," Brand said, and smiled wickedly at her. "One spoon."

And when their sundae came, and he leaned across

the table and fed her the cherry off their one spoon, something fizzed and crackled in the air between them, and she knew it was the very *something* she had always longed for.

Only what she hadn't expected was that it could be so powerful, would resist taming and would leave her heart feeling as if it had received a direct strike from a lightning bolt.

She didn't walk out of Maynard's. She floated out. And she floated through the rest of the weekend: helping him with his mother's roses the next day, talking on her front porch deep into the night.

They talked about small things: memories, shared acquaintances, the news that had made the paper that day. They talked of reclaiming rosebeds and what she was doing at work.

And they talked of bigger things: how his relationship with his father was slowly improving, and how the visit had reassured him his father was still more than capable of living independently.

Sophie loved hearing the gentleness and respect in Brand's voice when he talked about his dad. She felt only a little guilty that he hadn't figured out his father and her grandmother were a little more than friends, but given how the relationship between the two men was improving, she hoped Dr. Sheridan would tell his son soon.

Now it was Sunday afternoon, sizzling hot, a perfect day to get back on her schedule and go to Blue Rock. Only, somehow, for Sophie, everything was getting blurred. Was this still about letting the town know she was so over Gregg Harrison?

Or had it slipped into something completely different and far more exciting? And did Brand feel it, too?

He really seemed not to and appeared to be able to

refuse the temptation of her with baffling ease. Publicly, his romantic skills were dazzling. Privately, he assumed more of a big-brother role. Yet, still, Sophie could not remember when conversation, and companionship had been so satisfying, so absolutely fulfilling, like a sense of coming home to the place you belonged after a long time away.

But today, at Blue Rock, she was determined to make him notice her in a way he wasn't going to forget as soon as they were alone together.

Underneath a too-large men's T-shirt, she had on the teeniest bikini the law would allow.

She knew their plan was succeeding. She knew the whole town was talking about them, about Brand Sheridan and Sophie Holtzheim.

Now her goal had altered itself. She just wanted Brand to notice she had grown up. She wanted him to see her as a woman.

She could see he was slowly being charmed by the town he had left behind. But did that slow charming extend to her, too?

He picked her up in a four-wheel drive, a Jeep that looked like army surplus from the Second World War.

"Where's your car?"

"I traded it in. I like this one better. Better for loading boats."

Did that mean he was planning another fishing trip? Was he planning things with her? The way he was looking at her, no wonder the lines were blurring.

"I took a big hit for the boat scratch, though."

She walked around his new vehicle. The paint was nonexistent, the leather seats were cracked. But it had something wonderful about it. "I love it," she decided. "Very Indiana Jones."

He regarded her thoughtfully for a minute, shook his head. "You're serious, aren't you?"

"It just seems more you than the other one."

Blue Rock was a short hike in to a canyon, a back pool off the Blue River where the water was deep and still and a color of green that put emeralds to shame. A rocky beach lined the pool, and Blue Rock was an out-cropping on one side, providing a twelve-foot leap into the water. More cliffs loomed above Blue Rock, including the Widow Maker.

Already half the town was here seeking relief from the heat.

Sophie spread their blanket, aware of interest, aware of being watched. The rumors were starting to circulate, she knew.

And she suspected a lot of the talk was incredulous. What was a guy like him doing with a girl like her? Thanks to his father, people insisted on calling him a secret agent, thanks to her job, they insisted on seeing her as a librarian.

It did seem like the world's most unlikely combo!

But Sophie was about to prove she wasn't the girl everyone thought she was! She was about to break out of the mold the town had put her in ever since "What Makes a Small Town Tick."

She took a deep breath and yanked the T-shirt over her head.

And instead of feeling sexy, she instantly felt naked. In public.

Oh, God. Hadn't she had dreams that went like this?

CHAPTER SEVEN

INSTEAD of feeling sexy and powerful, Sophie couldn't even look at Brand, who had gone silent as the stones that rose around them.

"Race you," she said in a strangled tone, then ran for the water and dove in. It was a cool release from the heat of the day and the heat in her face.

But the bathing suit? Fragile at best, held together with spiderweb strings, it nearly parted company with her. And when she reached to tug it up into place, the fabric felt oddly mushy in her hand.

Brand had hit the water right behind her, and he came up, shaking droplets of water from the darkness of his hair and looking at her with a light in his eyes she had hoped to see.

But naturally, nothing in her world ever went as planned, especially in the courtship department. She had pictured that light in his eyes, had pictured them chasing each other around this pool like playful dolphins, had pictured him catching her....

She shook the vision away. She had to deal with reality. Treading water delicately, she said, "Brand, I'm in big trouble here."

The look on his face—the one she had dreamed of

since she was fifteen—was replaced instantly with concern. He reached for her. "What do you mean, big trouble?"

"Don't touch me."

"Excuse me. I assumed big trouble might mean you were about to drown."

"I think my bathing suit is disintegrating," she hissed at him. "Why is this my life?"

"Your bathing suit is disintegrating?" he asked with far more interest than sympathy.

"Why does everything go so wrong for me?" Even though she was whispering, it sounded like a wail. "Especially around you!"

"Hey, you can't blame me."

"Is it? Disintegrating?"

He was peering beneath the water.

"Don't look!"

"How the hell can I tell if it's disintegrating if I don't look?"

"Shh. I'm going to die of embarrassment."

"Nobody *dies* of embarrassment."

"Unfortunately." She tugged at the fabric. None of it actually seemed to be disintegrating. "Maybe it's not disintegrating. Melting. Imagine toilet paper getting wet."

"Sweet Pea?"

"What?"

"Sometimes swimsuits that, um, look like that one…"

Well, at least he'd noticed it before disaster struck!

"They aren't actually meant for swimming."

"What are you? The world's foremost expert on swimwear?"

"Unfortunately," he said.

She thought of him living on a yacht off the coast of

Spain. What had she been thinking, trying to impress him with skimpiness?

"Were you surrounded by beautiful women all the time?" she asked. She felt absurd, as though she was going to burst into tears. He was out of her league. He'd always been out of her league. She'd spent all this week forgetting that. Believing something else.

Believing the stupid fairy tales she'd sworn to leave behind.

And then, just like that, he made it all right.

He said, quietly and with utter conviction, "Not one of them was as beautiful as you, Sophie Holtzheim."

She trod water and stared at him. He wasn't laughing. He wasn't teasing. She couldn't look at what she saw in his face any longer or she was going to cry.

She glanced down and saw her new, sexy bathing suit, which had been bordering on indecent when dry, had definitely crossed the border now that it was wet. It was as translucent as a sheet of plastic wrap.

Then she did start to cry.

And, without a word, Brand gathered her to him, one arm locked around her, the other moving them toward shore. As soon as he could stand, his feet found the ground, and he wrapped both arms around her.

Under different circumstances she would have marveled at how his wet skin felt against her wet skin.

But under these circumstances, his body felt like a shield as he closed it around her. He lifted her, cradled her into his chest, carried her to their blanket. In one smooth move, he set her feet on the ground, ducked, flicked their blanket up off the rock and tucked it around her.

"I look like the same nerd as always," she said, sniffling.

He smiled. "That's what's beautiful about you." And

then, as if he had said way too much—as if he was the one who had been too revealing and not her—he did that annoying thing where he chucked her on the chin and turned and strode away.

He dove into the pool, crossed it in about four strong strokes and began to climb the rocks on the other side.

At first, Sophie thought it was part of her complete gift for everything going wrong around him. She'd weirded him out with her disintegrating bathing suit and her tears. He hadn't meant it about not one of those women from his other life being as beautiful as her. How could he have meant that?

But suddenly, it became clear to her.

He wasn't trying to escape her or her bathing suit or her tears.

He was doing what he always did. He was somehow making everything right. And he was doing it because he was climbing that cliff for her.

He went by the jut of Blue Rock without even pausing at it, without even acknowledging the teenage boys who were jostling for position there.

He began the more perilous climb, slower now, finding each foothold and each handhold, moving with confidence and purpose. How high above the water was that? Fifty feet?

She felt sick with dread and the absolute thrill of it.

And then, as he stood there on that precipice high above the pool, the one that hardly anyone had ever used before him or would use after him, the one they called the Widow Maker, he paused and looked down, not at the water below him but right at her. And he gave the sweetest little wave.

And that confirmed what he was doing. He was participating in that age-old dance—a man showing a woman that he would be the best, the strongest, the boldest.

He shouted, his voice, deep, sure, echoing off the canyon walls.

"Honor."

Not a person who heard that cry would not have shivers go up and down their spine.

Then he leapt, feet first, hands tucked at his sides, straight as an arrow, plummeting toward the water below him. His act of pure and foolish bravery did to Sophie what such feats of daring had done to women since the beginning of time: it filled her with fear for him, even as it did exactly what it was intended to do. Impressed her. Awed her. Evaporated whatever defenses she had remaining against him.

And it made her very happy she had found the nerve to wear the little white bikini—for her, every bit as bold as his leap from the cliff. Maybe once it was dry and not quite so see-through, she would uncover again. But for now, she was taking advantage of the fact that all eyes were on Brand to slip out from under the blanket and into her T-shirt.

He surfaced, tossed water from his hair, swam lazily across the pool, as if unaware every eye now followed him. He came and lay down on the blanket she had spread, right beside her, not even toweling off.

"Why did you shout 'Honor' before you jumped?" she asked.

"It's a battle cry. It's something worth fighting for. And dying for."

"It's more," she guessed softly. "It's about acknowledging your deepest self, isn't it, Brand? About acknowledging what is at your core, your highest and your best?"

"Ah, you're way too deep for a shallow guy like me, Sweet Pea." His eyes drifted over her lazily, with a possessiveness that made her mouth go dry.

"You know," he said, "we are both covered in scratches from those rosebushes. It makes it look like we've been up to all kinds of exciting things."

He reached out and traced one of the scratches on her arm.

"Like taming wild kittens?" she teased back, though the touch of his hand made her voice feel squeaky and breathless.

"Oh, yeah, I keep forgetting Sugar Maple Grove has a different standard for excitement than the rest of the world." He, thank God, seemed to lose interest in the scratch.

"In a way," she said, serious again, "for you, doing the dangerous thing, like jumping from that rock, is the safest thing of all, isn't it?"

"Huh?"

He was being deliberately obtuse. But she knew it. He had *felt* something when she had burst into tears. And by climbing up that cliff and throwing himself off that rock, he'd been able to feel something completely different instead.

"You engage yourself at a very physical level to avoid the risks and challenges of emotion."

"If that's a fancy way of saying guys don't like it when girls cry, uh, yeah. You got my number, Dr. Holtzheim. Not that it was that dangerous, even by Sugar Maple Grove standards."

"Apparently the standard is about to change," she said, watching as Martin, one of the more daring of the teenage boys who hung out here, started scrambling up the cliff straight toward the Widow Maker to the cheers of his friends.

He turned his attention from her to watch as the boy finally made it to the edge of the cliff. The boy hesitated and then jumped. His arms and legs windmilled furiously all the way down. He created a big splash, but surfaced, waving his two fingers in the V of victory.

Brand closed his eyes.

Sophie lay on their blanket, drowsing in the sun, staring at the water beading on the golden, perfect skin of the man who shared the blanket with her, his hair crusted with water diamonds, his eyes closed.

He looked so relaxed, and so at ease.

One week.

He'd only been home one week. How could her life feel so totally different? How could she feel so alive, as if energy tingled just below the surface of her skin all the time? And then, seeing him standing on the edge of the rock and seeing the truth about him finding safety in danger. It was as if she had unlocked a little secret about him.

And it probably felt so good because he did not reveal his secrets willingly.

"Mr. Sheridan?"

"Huh?" He rolled over, shielded his eyes from the sun.

"I'm Martin Gilmore."

Brand got to his feet, shook the young man's hand.

"That felt great. Jumping from the cliff." And then in a rush, "I'm thinking of joining the marines."

Without warning, the weariness that Sophie had not seen for days was back in Brand's eyes, the wall was up.

"Son, how old are you?"

"Seventeen."

Brand nodded and said quietly, "You should enjoy what you have here for as long as you can. Sophie, are you ready to go?"

She was surprised by the abruptness of it, but saw something in his face that did not invite argument.

She gathered up their picnic basket and blanket and he carried them to the Jeep, something remote in his face, untouchable.

"What just happened?" she asked him as they stood together at the open back of his vehicle, loading things in.

"Nothing happened," he said tersely, slamming the trunk shut.

"Yes, it did." She touched his arm, feeling him trying to move away from her. "What happened when Martin asked you about the marines?"

"I've zipped the body bag closed on too many kids that age."

"Tell me about that," she said quietly.

He scoffed. "Get real."

"No," she said, "tell me what you've seen and done."

"Sophie, you can't even handle a worm."

And that wall went back up so hard and so high she wondered if she'd been mistaken in thinking it had come down at all during the golden moments they had shared over the last week.

He shook off her arm, but she felt there was only one way to break the wall down. And she felt as if she *had* to, as if her life depended on reaching him and bringing him back here.

It wasn't like when she had kissed him in her office, launching herself at him, something to prove, an attempt to manipulate his impressions of her.

No, this was different.

It was a way of letting him know she could see him. She was coming for him, whether he liked it or not. He could jump off all the cliffs he liked, she was still coming, still going to find what was real about him.

She stood on tiptoes and touched her lips to his, tasted the sweet sting of the pure river water, the Razzle

Dazzle Raspberry cooler he had sipped earlier and the sweeter flavor of who he really was. Strong. Courageous. True. Deep.

Lonely.

Could you really know those things from touching your lips to someone else's? Not always.

But this time, yes.

He pulled back from her, and she knew he had gotten the message because she could see the wariness in his eyes.

"What was that about?" he growled.

"Mrs. Fleckenspeck was watching."

He turned and surveyed the wide and very empty gravel shoulder where everyone who used Blue Rock parked. "I don't see Mrs. Fleckenspeck. And what happened to rule number six hundred, no public demonstrativeness?"

"There weren't six hundred rules!" she said indignantly.

"There might as well not be any if you're just going to break them." He sounded grouchy, not at all like the man who had delivered sweet peas to her office, not like the one who had risked his neck racing her down Sugar Maple Grove's sleepy streets, nor the one who had chased her with worms or jumped off cliffs trying to impress her. Oh, she was beginning to get it!

He liked it when *he* was the one breaking the rules, when *he* was the one upsetting the apple cart.

"Okay," he said, looking everywhere but at her, "I think our duty here is done. Let's go."

And she never let on for a moment how disappointing she found that, or the fact that he drove fast all the way home, as if he couldn't put enough distance between them and what had happened.

She had sensed something real in all this pretense. Had sensed if he confided in her about the burdens he carried, it would get real in a brand-new way, a way neither of them would be able to step back from.

How long had it been since he had trusted someone with who he really was? Had he ever?

Good grief! It struck Sophie that there was a possibility that she was every bit as in love with Brand Sheridan as she had been at fifteen.

And that it was unlike loving Gregg. This kind of love could cost her everything.

Again.

Her whole world could be shattered all over again. Was she strong enough for that?

Brand could still taste the pure water of Blue Rock and the sweet invitation of Sophie's kiss when he crawled into bed that night.

Maybe *he* was going to have to write some rules. Like no more kissing, *ever.* But then she would know.

It awakened something in him. Something that burned. And yearned and ached. Something that was desperate for someplace soft and safe and blissful to rest his weary head. Sophie, just Sophie, never mind bikinis that melted in water, made him burn and yearn and ache.

He'd been back in sweet, sleepy Sugar Maple Grove for a week. And the astonishing truth was he had not been bored, not even once.

The knot of tension that had become a part of him had been slowly uncurling, relaxing. Until that kid at the swimming hole, a reflection of his younger self, no doubt a young man addicted to speed, reckless and restless, without a care in the world, and talking about throwing this world away. He wondered now why young men were so damned eager to leave all this behind them.

Think of something else, he ordered himself. So he did. He contemplated the fact that his father wasn't home.

Bingo at the St. James Hall tonight, Sophie had told him when they'd arrived back at the house to find his father's car missing.

"Dad's leading a pretty full life." More and more he felt content about his father's circumstances.

"Oh, yeah, well, good for him." But she'd looked away. Despite how he was managing to reassure himself, her reaction gave Brand the uneasy idea Sophie knew something about his father that she didn't want him to know. That had been evident when he'd asked her what she knew about the fire. Something had risen in her face—panic?

That was okay. He knew things he didn't want her to know, either.

Tell me what you have seen and done, she'd insisted, for the second time, and for the second time he had felt the terrible sway of temptation.

For a moment, temptation had made him see her, not as a child who needed his protection, but as a woman who could help him carry the burden.

He snorted to himself. He'd come back to Sophie against his desire to think of something—anything—else.

But since he was here, what kind of man asked a woman to help carry his burdens? Why was it he hadn't even known how heavy they were until she had asked him *what have you seen and done* and part of him had felt as if it would *die* if it didn't tell her.

Sinclair had had the right idea, he thought reaching for the letters that had been sent home to Sarah some sixty-five years ago.

Private Horsenell had now been overseas for months. His letters were becoming less frequent and far less revealing. The initial excitement and curiosity had given way to a faint overtone of cynicism. He was no longer in Ireland, but, in the early days of 1943, in the south of France.

My dearest Sarah, this one read,

Please do not hound me to tell you of the things I have done. Most of it is unpleasant. Truly, you do not want to know, and just as truly, I do not want to tell you.
I send my love,
Sinclair.

But the last line seemed to be written as an obligation.

It was evident Sinclair was manning up and keeping his secrets to himself, Brand thought, putting the letters away, not having the heart to look at any more of them tonight.

Still, even though he put them aside, Sinclair and Sarah haunted Brand over the decades that separated him from them. He thought of them even after he had turned out the light.

Sinclair was changing, whether he knew it or not. The man he had first been would have never written with such blunt impatience, "do not hound me." There was something hard in Sinclair that had not been there before, it had crept into the last four or five letters. Brand did not think it boded well for sweet little Sarah, sitting at home pining for a boy who no longer existed.

When Brand had raced Sophie on their bikes, felt the wind and the speed and the surprising challenge of beating her, he had been, for the first time in a long, long while, a boy he recognized from the past. That boy, some forgotten part of himself, was being coaxed more and more to the surface with every second he spent in Sugar Maple Grove, and every second he spent with Sophie.

And, just like Sarah, Sophie would be nothing but disappointed if she thought that boy could ever come back completely.

And so would he.

Maybe next time she asked *what have you seen and done,* he'd try out Sinclair's line. *Do not hound me.*

Through his open bedroom window, Brand heard a car pull up, doors slam. Voices. The voices, his father's and Hilde's, went into the backyard and, out of curiosity, Brand got up out of bed and went to the window.

His father and Sophie's grandmother were in the darkness of the yard, leaning into each other, holding hands.

Then they kissed. Not a little peck on the cheek kind of kiss, either.

He pulled away from the window, feeling guiltily like a Peeping Tom. Brand felt astounded by what he had just witnessed and amazed by how angry it made him.

His father thought he had dishonored his mother by not coming to the funeral? How about replacing her so quickly, moving on to someone else as if she had not mattered at all?

He remembered Sophie's expression when they had talked about his father, and thought, *she knows.*

A betrayal. A good thing to remember the next time he was feeling tempted to trust her with his secrets.

He felt bitterly disappointed. Why? He was cynical by nature. He knew people disappointed each other. He was the foolish one for feeling as if he could trust Sophie with his life. And his secrets. Thank God he had not given in to the temptation to tell her anything tonight, though the urge to do so had been momentarily almost overwhelming.

He felt a startling desire to escape from this situation, to run.

But he was not a man who had ever run away from things that weren't easy. He had invited them. He had taken up his fighter's stance and invited the world to give him its best shot. The military had taken his restlessness and his recklessness and turned him into a gladiator who entered the arena willingly.

Every arena, he realized, except this one.

He had never before entered the arena of the human heart. Sophie had been so right by that pool today.

He found safety in danger. Danger engaged him physically. It gave him the rush of feeling intensely alive without the risk of engaging his heart.

Now he was aware of standing on a precipice far more dangerous to him than the Widow Maker could ever be.

He was falling in love with Sophie.

Falling was an accident. Jumping was a choice. No wonder he was so guarded against love. It had happened without his permission and without his planning. There was an element of being powerless to it. And in his world, being powerless was a weakness.

Mentally, he stepped back from the precipice. Mentally, he took charge.

He would finish fixing his mother's rosebeds, he vowed. That's how he would honor her, even if his father was incapable of it. And then he would confront his father about the new relationship.

And then he would go. His unit kept temporary quarters in California. He had not lived in barracks since he was a young pup, but he could go there until other arrangements were made.

Brand took out the cell phone he had not used for an entire week and sent a text message to his sister. "Dad seems fine." He hesitated. Did he add, "He has a new friend"? No. That was his dad's business.

Then Brand sent a text to his boss. He couldn't stay here for a month. It was no longer the safest place in the world.

It had become the most dangerous.

Something had happened. He had fallen. For his hometown. For Sophie.

But he doubted he could ever come back here, to this way of life, not anymore than Sinclair Horsenell could come back here. They had something in them now that these small towns could not handle. And that nothing in a small-town girl's experience prepared her for—a man who was cynical. Jaded.

Damaged in a way that could not be repaired. Not by all that charm, not by all that innocence.

Not by all the love in the world.

What about his commitment to help Sophie hold her head up high again? To make it look to the whole town as though he was romancing her? He had tossed her schedule beside his bed and now he looked at it.

There was only one more thing. The engagement party of her ex-fiancé. If he went and broke both Slick Harrison's legs it would be a nonissue.

The kind of man who had thoughts like that could never have a girl like Sophie.

Besides, if there was one thing he had always counted on himself to be, it was a man of his word. His four-year undercover assignment had made him doubt that part of himself, now he felt it was imperative he get it back.

He had told Sophie he would help her out. Just because she was part of the conspiracy of silence around his father's romantic life, did that let him off the hook?

No. Brian Lancaster would never have done the honorable thing. And Brand knew, at some instinctual level, that getting himself back after four years of pretending to be someone else meant behaving with honor. And integrity.

Even when it hurt. But not when it hurt Sophie. Except it *was* going to hurt her, because he'd take her to the damn party, but until then, he was avoiding her completely.

Because he could keep on getting in deeper with her and hurt her a lot later, or start pulling back and hurt her a little now.

He was pulling back and it was for her own good.

CHAPTER EIGHT

THE dress had been a last-ditch attempt to fix something that was broken. Sophie Holtzheim had never owned a dress like the one she was wearing. Not even that wedding gown she had donned, unbelievably, only two weeks ago, did what this dress did.

Iridescent green silk, the dress was the first time Sophie had ever splurged on a designer label.

Now, she could clearly see why people did.

The dress didn't just adore the female body, it worshipped it. The dress was ten times sexier than that bikini had been, which seemed impossible, given the differences in the amount of fabric, but, nonetheless, it was true.

This dress floated around her, a whisper of sensuality. It delicately hugged certain assets, celebrating the sensuous curves of her breasts and hips.

The color and the fabric made Sophie's skin look as smooth and flawless as a glass pitcher of heavy cream. The length, ending just above her knee, made her legs look slender and endless.

And the shimmering color brought out something spectacular in her eyes. Well, the dress, and an hour of makeup instruction at the local cosmetics counter!

Still, Sophie was aware that all the hopes she had

invested in this dress, that it could fix something broken, were not justified. And the *something broken* was not her reputation in Sugar Maple Grove, either. She didn't care if Gregg Harrison fell in his own swimming pool because she looked so spectacular. That was no longer what she needed to fix—she didn't give a hoot about the town's perceptions of her.

It would not fix whatever had gone wrong between her and Brand.

She knew it the instant she went to the door and saw him standing on the stoop, breathtaking in a tux, the shirt the most pristine white, the bow tie perfectly knotted, because the look on his face when he saw her did not change from the look she had been putting up with on his face ever since they had been to Blue Rock nearly a week ago.

All week, he had been coolly distant. When she had showed up at his rosebed, ready to work, he had announced it was really a project he wanted to do himself, to honor his mother. *It's personal.*

That was not something you could really argue with.

But she soon found out it was not just the rose garden. He didn't want to go fishing, either. Or to the movies. He didn't want to ride their bikes downtown for ice cream.

Point blank: he didn't want to be with her.

If she'd had an ounce of pride she would have canceled tonight, but dammit, from the start it had been all about tonight. This was the point: to make it public that she was so over Gregg.

And naturally, she had hoped the dress would sway Brand.

But she could see instantly that it had failed.

When her grandmother came to the door to see them

off, she said, in German, "See if he can dance, Sophie. There is nothing like a man who can dance."

And he said to her grandmother, his German perfect, much better than Sophie's, "I'm afraid I am no dancer."

Her grandmother actually looked pleased that he spoke German, as if it troubled her not a bit that he had been eavesdropping on what they had assumed were private conversations since his arrival. Embarrassed, Sophie reviewed some of the things her grandmother had said, tried to remember her responses.

But maybe it wasn't the details that mattered so much as the deliberateness of his deception. Sophie felt something shiver along her spine, and, looking at his carefully schooled features, she thought maybe she didn't know him at all.

They walked down the walk and he held open the car door for her—he'd borrowed his father's vehicle for tonight—and closed it quietly after her, with all the polite remoteness of a paid escort.

Which, in a way, he was. Just a guy doing a gal a favor. She was the one who had let the boundaries blur, she was the one who'd begun to bring expectations, she was the one who had read way too much into stolen kisses, shared laughter, physical awareness, a daring leap from a rock.

"We need to discuss the breakup," he said as he took the driver's seat, pulled away from the curb smoothly.

Since she felt what they needed to discuss was the fact he spoke German and had never once admitted it, she was not prepared for that.

Even though she knew the dress had not worked, even though all week she had felt something slipping away from her, even though she had an unsettling sense of not knowing who he was *at all,* Sophie felt unprepared for that. Completely.

"Excuse me?"

"The breakup," he repeated. "If I just leave and never come back it's just going to look like you've been ditched again. That was hardly the point of this whole exercise."

"Are you leaving?"

"Yes."

"I thought you were staying for a month."

"You can't count on a guy in my line of work, Sophie." This was said harshly.

"You're never coming back?"

He glanced at her, then looked straight ahead. He didn't answer.

Which she took to mean he was never coming back. How could she feel so bereft? They were supposed to be playing. Pretending.

But she had caught a glimpse of the truth. She loved him as much as she had when she was fifteen.

And she was going to be just as devastated now as she was then. When he left Sugar Maple Grove.

She wanted to wail at him, *How could you never come back?*

Instead she thought, I only have a little while longer to convince him this is a place worth coming back to.

That I am a girl worth coming back to.

"We don't have to have a public breakup," she said, not looking at him, looking out the window. "I can pretend we're talking on the phone, e-mailing for a while And then just let it fizzle out after a few months."

"Make sure it looks like it's you who let it fizzle," he said. "Tell people my job was just too demanding. It *is* too demanding for a woman who wants the things that you want."

"What do you think I want?"

"It's written all over you what you want." His voice

had an edge to it. "A little house like that one right there," he nodded at a house they were driving by, a play set in the yard, with a baby swing and a regular swing.

"Sandboxes and tricycles," he said in a low voice. "A husband who is home at night. Picnics and fried chicken on Sunday. The kind of life Sugar Maple Grove lends itself to."

"Are you saying that you won't ever settle down, Brand? That you don't eventually want those things out of life, too?"

"My job destroys relationships," he said grimly. "I've seen it happen a dozen times. It's not fair to ask anyone to share a life that is full of unpredictability and constant risk."

"That sounds so lonely."

"I'm not lonely," he snapped, and something about the way he said it made her look at him and think, *yes, he is.*

But she had already done her best to lure him in from his lonely world. For a while she had convinced herself she could. Now, glancing over at him, she saw the formidable will of the man. She saw that he had decided what he wanted, and that Sugar Maple Grove was not part of that. And neither was she. She wondered if she had ever known him at all.

But, for all the pain she felt, Sophie knew she had learned something real and something important. Two weeks in the company of Brand Sheridan had made Gregg seem like a cardboard cutout of a man that she had tucked in beside her to make her feel as if she was really experiencing a relationship, when, in fact, she had settled for a cheap imitation.

How was that for an irony? This relationship—the pretend one—felt real, whereas her real relationship had felt pretend.

At her instructions they left Sugar Maple Grove behind them and traveled a twisty country road until they reached the impressive gate of the Harrison estate. A sign swung in a gentle breeze. Today it had lavender balloons on it, to match the ugly theme of the invitation, Sophie thought sourly.

"Pheasant Corpse Estate," he read the sign out loud, his voice heavy with cynicism.

"*Copse,* not *corpse!*"

"Whatever. Wow. Do they give themselves titles, too? The Duke and Duchess of Dead Pheasant Estate?"

"This is where I was going to live," Sophie said, reacting to his sarcasm, feeling defensive, as if he was criticizing *her,* her dreams.

She remembered how she used to feel as she drove up the long, winding, tree-lined drive. It curved through a little forest and past a stream, and then opened up into a grove where a grand house was located.

The house had once been a two-story farmhouse, but clever additions over the years gave it the fairy-tale look of the country estate written on the gate. The shingle siding had been recently stained in a lovely dove-gray, the white of the porches and shutters and trim gleamed with fresh paint.

She used to feel as if this was a safe place. As if, finally, after the deaths of her parents, all was going to be well with her world again. She was going to be part of a family. She was going to have a place to call home in a way her house had never been since her parents had left it.

She realized it was the loss of that vision that she had mourned as much as the loss of her relationship with Gregg. Perhaps more so.

And then Sophie realized, shocked, that for her the danger was in choosing safety. This was the place designed to protect her heart after the deaths of her parents. In safety was the danger she would stagnate, never discover her true potential, never live fully.

Tonight the house was lit from within, every light on, spilling gold out huge paned-glass windows over the sweep of the front lawns.

"You can pull around to the back," she said with unconscious familiarity. He did, and, as she had guessed, cars were being parked between the house and the barn. Not that the barn housed animals. It had been turned into storage for vintage cars a long time ago.

As they drove past the back of the house, Sophie could see that the stone patio was already overflowing with guests, that gas lights winked off the turquoise water of the swimming pool.

"Let me get this straight. You were going to live with his parents?" he asked, finding a parking spot on the far side of the barn, a good distance for her to walk in the three-inch stiletto heels of the shoes that had set off the dress so perfectly.

"We weren't going to live with his parents. There's a suite."

Brand made a growling noise.

"His brother lived there until he got established, too." She recognized something even more defensive in her voice.

He cut the engine, and when she reached for the handle of her door, he gave her a dark look. She sat back, waited.

He came around to her door, opened it, offered her his arm.

"You were going to live with his parents," he said with disgust.

She would rather not have taken his arm, but the

ground was uneven, and she was feeling a little wobbly on the shoes.

"I don't see anything wrong with that," she said stiffly.

"*You* wouldn't."

She could hear laughter, tinkling of glasses, voices as they approached the back lawn, the terraces. It occurred to her she did not feel one ounce of trepidation about seeing Gregg. Or his fiancée. Not one.

"What's wrong with it?" she demanded. "Living with his parents until we got established?"

But she already knew. It was *safe*. And she hated it that he could see that so clearly.

"What's wrong with it? What about running around naked? What about making love in the backyard under the stars? And on the kitchen table? What about passion taking you so hard you scream with it? Sob his name. Beg him to make you feel as if the universe is exploding?"

He wasn't even trying to keep his voice down.

The world he was painting—a world governed by passion instead of safety—filled her with a kind of agony. She fiercely longed to know the wild part of her that her need for safety had prevented her from ever discovering, ever knowing.

But she had never wanted to feel anything like that with Gregg. Or with any other man. She wanted to feel those things with him. With Brand.

Even as his words stirred something wild in her, a longing, she recognized that Brand, usually so controlled, sounded very angry, angrier that she had ever seen him.

And she realized she felt angry herself.

"Don't you miss any of that, Sophie?"

"But not with you, of course." Her voice snapped. It felt as though the anger exploded in her. How dare he bring her to the brink of all life could be and then abandon her there with her heart full of this terrible longing, her body nearly quivering with it?

For a moment he went very still. He stopped and took a deep breath. He looked at her, hard, and she could see he had seen the dress, and her. And that it had had exactly the effect she had wanted. With a man less determined, maybe it could have fixed whatever was broken between them. Maybe it could have taken them to that place of pure passion, where reason was given a rest.

But Brand looked away from her, shoved his hands in his pockets, rocked back on the heels of his shoes and studied the star-studded sky, gathering himself, gathering his strength.

And she knew why. He was about to tell her good-bye. He was doing his duty, escorting her to the party. But it was really good-bye and it had been for a week now.

"You always knew we were pretending," he said quietly. "That was our deal. You always knew it would never be me that chased you around the kitchen table until you were breathless."

She yanked her arm out of the crook of his. "So nothing about this time here has been true, Brand. Nothing?"

He hesitated, her heart flew up in hope, and then fell like a bird with an arrow through it when he said coldly, "Nothing."

"You," she spat out, "are the most dishonest man I have ever met."

"Don't even get me going about honesty," he said.

"Really? That's funny. I don't remember tricking *your* elderly grandmother."

"Your elderly grandmother who is out in my back-yard kissing the daylights out of my newly widowed father?"

"You entertained yourself at our expense!"

"And you knew about my dad. You knew about my dad and your grandmother. And you never said a word."

"For your information," Sophie said, biting out each word, her enunciation perfect, for once not stumbling all over herself, "your Dad is twice the man you'll ever be. He's not afraid."

"Yeah, like I'm afraid."

"Your dad is not afraid of love."

He was silent for a moment, and then said, "Are you telling me he *loves* your grandmother?"

"Ask *him*," she snapped, "and you know what? Forget the gentle breakup. Forget the e-mails and the slow fizzle. In fact, forget we were ever together."

She didn't care that her voice was rising, and that people close to the edge of the lawn had turned toward them. "Forget this whole shameful sham. Because you know what, Brand Sheridan? I don't need *you* so I can hold *my* head up high!"

And then she walked away from him.

It was disastrous, of course. A heel turned over on the uneven ground of the driveway.

When he walked toward her, looking like he was going to offer his big strong arm—rescue his clumsy little sweet pea one last time—she cast him a withering look, took the shoes off and walked in her stockings over the gravel toward the lights and noises of a party she didn't dread in the least.

Brand watched her go, her shoes in her hand, sashaying down that drive without a glance back at him.

It was a moment he had somehow lived for: to see finally that she didn't need him anymore. He had seen the truth in the furious light that had sparked in her eyes right now.

Sophie Holtzheim could make it on her own. She

was like a tiny bird who had fallen from the nest, and he had picked her up, stroked her feathers until she was ready to fly.

And it seemed to him, seeing her in that dress tonight, he had never seen a woman more ready to fly.

He just hadn't expected to feel quite so sad to have to let her go.

He watched her for a moment longer, then, unable to resist, he made his way to the edge of the lawn, aware this might be the last time he ever saw her.

The patio was crowded, but he picked her out of the crowd instantly. It wasn't just the dress—that impossibly sexy, fantastic dress—that set her apart, though it did. It was the way she carried herself, like a queen.

The confidence, her sense of herself, was radiating from her. He could see in the way people looked at her that they noticed it.

He watched her until she got to the bar.

He was not sure how, over all that noise, he heard her. But he did.

"Whiskey on the rocks. Make it a double."

Even ten minutes ago he would have told her to take it easy. Now, it was clear his days of telling her anything were over.

The way she looked tonight, gorgeous, glorious, *on fire,* it occurred to him that his first night back here, he really had seen a goddess in the garden. She just hadn't known it yet. And maybe she didn't see yet what he saw so clearly.

He stood there for a moment, in awe of the woman she would become. Soon, every guy in the place would be all over her. They would be bringing her drinks and asking her to dance, later they would probably get bolder and try to coax her into the shadows to steal kisses from her.

And from the look on her face, she wouldn't have one bit of trouble handling them.

And if she did, if she floundered with this new power she would have over men, it was not his problem. She was not a little girl anymore. He was not her protector.

She didn't need him.

As he thought of that, he felt a void open up in him that could never, ever be filled.

He stood at the edge of the crowd for a moment longer and then, before she could see him watching her, he turned and walked away.

Brand let himself back into his father's house quietly, went under the sloped roof of his boyhood room, checked his messages.

Arrangements were in place: check the unit office when he got to California, he would be given temporary accommodations and a temporary assignment, teaching new recruits to FREES the techniques of very advanced rope rescues.

That was his life. If for a while, here in Sugar Maple Grove, he'd forgotten that, it didn't really matter. So, he'd fallen.

You picked yourself up, you dusted yourself off and you got on with it. You didn't look back, either.

He packed his bag, hoping to slip out unnoticed, not ready to confront his father, but of course, this was the one night his father was home.

"I thought you took Sophie to that party."

"I did. She didn't need me to stay. Dad, I have to go back to work."

"Tonight?"

"It's sudden, I know."

"You fought with Sophie," his father said, watching him.

"It wasn't a fight."

"You promised her you'd help her hold her head up high."

"In the end she figured out no one can help you with that."

"You didn't hurt her, did you?"

"Less now than I might have later."

"Ah." His father watched him, sighed. "You know. About me and Hilde."

"The path worn out between the two houses gave you away."

"There's nothing to give away. I'm not ashamed."

"Really? Then why didn't you just tell me?"

"I didn't expect *you* to understand. I knew you'd be angry, and you are."

Brand said a word he'd never said in front of his father before, watched the doctor flinch from it.

"There's no need to be vulgar," his father said.

"I'm a rough man in a rough profession," Brand said. "You never let me forget that. That I let you down by choosing my own life. I've been a constant disappointment to you. The funeral just cemented how you felt anyway."

His father looked stunned. "Brand, that's not—

Brand held up his hand. "You couldn't or wouldn't forgive me because I couldn't come home for her funeral, as if I'd betrayed the thing that mattered most to me. And all that time, while you were judging me, you couldn't even wait a decent amount of time before you replaced my mother? Yeah, I guess you could say I'm angry."

"Sophie told me about the work you were doing, that other people might have been hurt or killed if you came home."

"Sophie shouldn't have needed to tell you that," he

said stiffly. "It might have been nice if you just believed the best of me."

"I'm sorry."

Brand was not sure he had ever heard his father say those words. Certainly not to him.

"Dad, how long after Mom died before this started?"

"Stop. Don't make it cheap and tawdry, and most of all don't make it disrespectful of your mother."

"How can I make it anything else?"

"This is what you don't get," his father said, softly, something broken in his voice. "Life is short, Brand. When it offers you something good, you don't always get a second chance at it.

"I loved your mother. Maybe you can live without love in your life. It seems you can. You're still at that age where you regard time as endless, something that never runs out. If you pass on something, well, heck, there's lots of time to get back to it later. But I saw time run out with your mother, how quickly it can happen, without an ounce of warning."

"I've seen time run out, too." Brand said.

His father looked at him, seemed to see him maybe for the first time in many, many years. His expression was concerned. "I guess you have, Brandon. I guess you've seen some terrible things. A father wants to protect his children from those things, but I couldn't protect you. You were always so headstrong, always moved away from what I wanted for you.

"All I'm trying to say is that if things follow the natural order, I don't have as much time left as you. I don't want to waste a minute of what I have left mourning things gone so intensely that I toss the gift God is trying to give me, now, back in His face.

"I don't know if you can understand that or not."

But the thing was, Brand could understand it. He even envied the fact his father could make the choice he himself was incapable of making.

"I have to go."

"Are you going back to do something dangerous?" his father asked, and Brand could see so clearly what love did. It made people afraid for the ones they loved. It confirmed the wisdom of his walking away from his dad, from Sugar Maple Grove, from Sophie.

Was he going back to do something dangerous? *Probably.* If not sooner, later. But he didn't say that. He said, "Nah. I think they're sticking me in training for a while."

And the relief on his father's face made that final act of protecting him worth the lie.

And after only three days instructing, Brand was sent on an assignment. He didn't even have time to unpack his bags. It was a military mission that used all his physical and linguistic skills. Sophie had been so right. In this sense of urgency and danger and mission, Brand felt safest.

An operative was caught in a foreign jail; their mission was to free him at whatever cost. The operation required training, discipline, precision and timing. It was physically highly dangerous, it was fast. It was the perfect antidote to the soft mission he'd spent four years on.

But it wasn't the perfect antidote for his loneliness. Danger and adrenaline did not give him the escape he had come to expect. They did not fill the spaces. They felt, oddly, like cheap imitations of what real feeling felt like.

He'd known a different kind of rush now.

He'd known the rush of racing bikes down Main Street in Sugar Maple Grove. He'd known the pure delight of bailing out a leaky boat with Sophie. He'd had the rush of that out-of-control feeling of *falling*.

Falling for Sophie.

And now, he practiced the discipline of a man who wanted to taste more but forced himself to walk away. For her. For her own good.

Now he had to put away those days of perfect summer. He needed to set up his life again. A place of his own, close to base but off base. He needed to fill his minutes with busy work so that he would not even think of her, not give in to the temptation to call her just to hear the sound of her voice.

Couldn't I? Couldn't I just call? Just once? To see how she is?

As he was unpacking the few things he owned, he came to the duffel bag that he had taken to Sugar Maple Grove.

At the very bottom of it were the letters from Sinclair Horsenell. He realized as he thumbed through them that he had read all of them.

Except one.

He opened it now. It was dated the beginning of May 1944. Private Horsenell did not know that D-day and the end of the war loomed large, but Brand did.

Dear Sarah,
I am writing you with the most unhappy of intentions. It is my wish to discontinue our engagement. Please do not think it is about you, for it is not.

It is about me. I am not the boy who left you. I have become a man I do not know, whom you would not recognize. I have seen and done things of such a horrible nature they are written on my soul.

How can I come back to the world I remember but can no longer belong in? How can I come back to you?

I urge you to find a man who did not come to this place, who was too young to give himself to this violent struggle, or who was an only son who stayed home and farmed his land. I urge you to find a man who has retained a gentle and considerate manner that is worthy of you.

I urge you to find a man who does not wake in the night screaming, who has not had the blood of his fellow man splash into his face, who will not carry the stench and the cries of the dying to his grave.

With my gravest best wishes for you, always,

Sinclair Horsenell.

And Brand knew, after he put that letter away, that he would not phone Sophie. That the very choice to be a warrior had excluded him from what he had vowed to spend his life protecting.

His choices had changed him. Made him a man who could not accept love because of the price others would have to pay in order to love him. He had seen that in the relief in his father's face when he had lied to him, telling him there was no danger in what he would do next.

Sophie would be better off, just as Sinclair had said to Sarah, to find a man who was not haunted by the things he'd done, a man who knew no other realities beyond the one of Sugar Maple Grove.

Brand had scorned Gregg Hamilton, but what if that was exactly the kind of man Sophie needed?

"Maybe one not content to live with his parents," he muttered out loud.

And yet, when he thought of those things he had said to her that last night, he hated it that it would not be him. Hated it.

He knew he would make himself crazy if he did not leave the sweet summer madness that had struck him in his hometown behind him. For good. No looking back. No "what ifs," no regrets. No asking about her when he talked to his father. No surfing the Internet to follow threads with her name in them.

But for all that he was resolute, it seemed that, like Sinclair, Brand wanted Sophie to know it wasn't about her. Sinclair had said it eloquently. So, he would have one last contact. Not in person. Not even by phone.

But just so she knew it was not about her.

These letters did not belong to him, anyway. They belonged to the history of a small town. And when she read them, she would understand. He was a warrior who could not go home.

But in the end, he could not resist the temptation to send her not one thing, but two. He sent her that packet of letters, and he phoned the art gallery on Main Street in Sugar Maple Grove and arranged to have a painting sent to her, a painting of an old red boat tied to the end of a dock….

When he sent those letters he didn't feel, not like a warrior, he felt like a weakling. And like the loneliest man on the planet.

Then it hit him like a bolt of lightening.

He loved her.

He loved Sophie Holtzheim.

Enough to protect her from the worst thing that could happen in that nice safe cozy world she had made for herself. Loving him back.

Hours later his phone rang. There had been a hostage taken by a terrorist cell in a faraway land. The hostages were being held on the thirty-first floor of what had once been a posh hotel.

It was, of course, getting international press coverage, so his boss was concerned about sending him. Because of Chop-Looey, they didn't want him photographed. On the other hand, they needed their best climber, one with the skill to get in and out of a hotel window thirty-one stories off the ground.

Brand didn't give a hoot about the press being there. He had to do that job. And he had to be realistic. Some of the hostages might not survive the rescue. He might not. And that was the type of thing that he never, ever, wanted to bring home to someone like Sophie.

CHAPTER NINE

In the days after Brand left Sugar Maple Grove, Sophie discovered that anger had an energy to it that was far preferable to self-pity, even the righteous self-pity of a heartbreak.

She had never been an angry person, but in those days after Brand departed, Sophie made up for lost time. Every time she thought of him, and that was with unfortunate frequency, she found she felt so much better if she wrecked something.

She had a pile of snapped pencils at her desk, shredded papers, two coffee cups with no handles, a shattered plate and a heap of twisted-beyond-repair paper clips.

She had punched the numbers on her calculator so hard she'd had to junk it, jammed her printer trying to force the ink and wrecked her stapler purposely trying to pound staples through too many papers as she spat out his name.

She felt furious with him: for leaving, for making her love him, for ruining her last-ditch effort to put together her shattered dreams, a task she now recognized to be as futile as trying to put together Humpty Dumpty after his tumble from the wall.

By week two, it had stopped being fun breaking things, but her anger was unabated.

Only now, Sophie didn't direct it at Brand.

She directed it where it belonged. At herself.

She'd been the one who had believed she needed someone else in order to hold her head up high.

That was what had gotten her into trouble with Gregg in the first place.

And her anger at herself drove her forward; she wasn't being that girl who waited for a man to protect and rescue her anymore. She was not going to be the girl she had been with Gregg—waiting helplessly and hopelessly for him to change his mind.

She was not waiting. She had wasted quite enough of her life moping. No, she was learning to protect and rescue herself. Sophie signed up for self-defense classes three evenings a week at Sebring's Gym in the neighboring town. In the same gym, they had a rock wall, and they offered climbing instruction, so she signed up for that, too.

It was time to find her own strength!

The third week after Brand had left, it hit her that he really wasn't coming back. And he wasn't phoning, or sending any e-mails, either. There was no sense rushing home to check the blinks on her answering machine, there was no sense rushing to work to check her e-mails.

As the longest, hottest summer in the history of Sugar Maple Grove drew to a close, she bought a new bathing suit. Not some ridiculous piece of film and fluff that melted in the water, either!

No, a one-piece, plain black, with a sturdy racer back. She celebrated who she intended to become by going to Blue Rock by herself. She dropped her towel and swam across the inky-green water of the pool.

She ignored the temptation to relive something that was done, to remember being here with him, to remember his words that she had been the most beautiful of them all, and she began to climb.

She stopped at Blue Rock.

This is good enough, she told herself, *high enough, a great enough demonstration of courage and independence.* But it wasn't. She turned her back on Blue Rock and began the treacherous climb to the Widow Maker.

Her limbs were trembling from exertion when she finally pulled herself onto that last outcrop of rock.

Her nerve was gone completely, but the horrible truth was that she was more afraid to try and pick her way back down the rocks than to jump.

She stood at the edge. Her heart beat in her throat. Her hands were slick with the sweat of pure panic. What if she didn't jump out far enough and caught a rock on the way down? What if she slipped while she was trying to launch, and fell instead of jumping? What if she twisted in the air, and landed wrong and really, really hurt herself?

"I do have a gift for things going wrong," she reminded herself.

Now people gathered at the pool had started to notice she was up here. She saw several shielding their eyes against the sun that was bright on her back.

Jump, she ordered herself. All her muscles coiled, but fear held her back. She did that half a dozen more times. Now everyone down below was watching her. The sun was sinking at her back.

If she didn't do something soon, she was going to be up here all night. A laughingstock, *again.* A rescue crew might have to be called.

What if word got back to him? That she was a chicken?

No! How was she going to live with herself if she was a chicken.

Jump, she told herself. Only this time it was different.

She heard a voice whisper, *Sophie, I know who you really are.*

Who was it? Brand? Her father? Her mother? His mother?

Whoever it was, the fear evaporated, and she whispered, "Honor."

And then she stepped off the end of the earth with absolute faith in who she really was.

The tumble through the air was remarkably brief. The water, when she hit it, felt like concrete. She plummeted through it, her feet actually touched the bottom of the deep, deep water of the canyon of Blue Rock.

She shoved off it, broke the surface.

The people who had watched her were clapping and cheering. And she was laughing.

Because it had been so much easier than she had expected. What she had suspected about Brand Sheridan was all too true. The kind of courage it took to fling yourself off a rock into the pool below was nothing in comparison to the kind of courage it took to leave your heart vulnerable in a cruel world.

On week four she bought a motorcycle.

And squeezed in lessons to learn to ride it between rock-climbing and self-defense. Her self-defense instructor asked her out. So did a man she met at the climbing wall. She said no, but she was pleased nonetheless.

Just when she told herself she was completely over him, over Brand Sheridan, forever and for always, the painting arrived.

She didn't like it the way she once had. It no longer seemed like an invitation to spend a quiet perfect summer day with a fishing pole in the company of someone you cherished. It seemed a lonely picture, a choice *not* made. A life lived elsewhere, while the boat and the pond waited for people who never came. She put the painting in a closet where she didn't have to look at it.

She told herself that was how completely she was over him. Even his gifts could not cause a flood of sentimental longing in her.

But then the letters arrived. The painting didn't even have a note, the letters a brief one.

Sorry, I seem to have packed these by accident. They belong to you.

Just as with the painting, she wanted to dismiss the longing his being in touch created in her. She almost turned the letters over to Bitsy.

But something stopped her.

He had said the letters belonged not to the historical society but to *her.*

She put them in her bag, and that night, in the sanctuary of her own bed, she began to read. The letters read like a novel, and it was deep in the night before she got to the last one.

She didn't want to read it. She didn't want to know. But she had to read it. She had to know.

When she finished the last letter, she was sobbing.

Surely Sinclair had come back and married Sarah? Surely this last letter had not really been the end?

One thing Sophie was good at was researching history. By the closing of her office the next day, she knew the entire horrible truth.

On old microfiche from the *Sugar Maple Grove Gazette,* she found the banns that had been posted on January 1947 between Sarah Sorlington and Michael

Smith. Then she found the write-up for the wedding of Sarah and Michael, not of Sarah and Sinclair, dated June of the same year.

Sophie could barely read it through her tears.

"The bride wore ivory silk and carried forget-me-nots."

Forget-me-nots? Because they matched her eyes, or because she could not forget him, even as she married someone else?

Sophie cried even harder when she found the obituary for Sinclair Horsenell. She cried for a man who had died years before she was born, died alone in an old-soldiers' home. He had never married. He was survived by brothers and sisters and nieces and nephews, but no wife. No children.

Up until then she had thought she was over her angry phase. But after she read about Sinclair dying alone, she went to the secondhand store next door to the Historical Society and bought a whole box of dishes.

That night, in the Historical Society's concrete bunker of a basement she threw every one of those dishes against the wall. Even when she had broken every dish in that box, her fury had not abated. She was furious at Sinclair for being so stupid and stubborn, but she was way more furious at Sarah.

What kind of selfish, weak-minded girl could not read between the lines of that last letter and see the lonely desperation of a young soldier who had lost himself?

That poor man had lost faith in himself, and he had lost his way back to all the things he had once taken for granted. Where had Sarah been? Why hadn't she gone to him and brought him the map that would lead them home?

And then, sitting there in the rubble of the broken dishes, she knew, suddenly, with quiet certainty, why Brand had sent these letters back to her.

And it wasn't because they were the property of the Historical Society.

It was because he was a man who lived with the loneliness of having seen and done things that set him apart from the people he loved.

Like Sinclair Horsenell, he did not trust that anyone had kept the memory of who he really was alive and strong. Like Sinclair, he did not logically see how he could find his way home.

Suddenly she knew that's what it had all been about: the self-defense class, the rock-climbing, the leap from the Widow Maker, the purchase of the motorbike.

It had all been about being the woman who wasn't afraid to go get him, even if that meant following him into hell to bring him back.

It was about believing that love, not logic, would provide the map that would show both of them the way home.

She heard that voice again, the one she had heard on the rock. The one that had said, *Sophie, I know who you really are.*

And she recognized who spoke those words. Not Brand. Not her father. Not her mother. Not his mother.

It was the voice of her deepest self, her soul.

And it knew exactly who she was, and exactly what she needed to do.

Brand was exhausted. And heart-sore. It had already been too late for two of the hostages by the time FREES got on scene.

He walked up the stairs toward his apartment and went still. The lights in his suite were on. Had he left in such a hurry he'd left the lights on? Possible, though not likely. The press had been ordered not to show his face, but who knew?

As he drew closer he heard music.

The hair on the back of his neck rose, then settled. No bad guy—some remnant of Looey's operation who had spotted him because of the press coverage of the hotel hostage rescue—was sitting in there waiting for him with the lights on and the music blaring.

Still, he went up the steps quietly, reached for his key above the door molding. It was gone. The door was ajar. He stood to one side of the door, tilted his head, looked in.

He had a direct line of sight through the whole tiny apartment, except for the bedroom. There was a suitcase just inside the door.

And then he saw Sophie Holtzheim in his kitchen. The rush he felt was way different than the one he had felt being lowered off the hotel roof down to the thirty-first floor.

She looked amazing in a white tailored shirt, snug jeans, sandals. Her hair looked as if it had been cut, not short, but styled. It looked glossy and glorious, it begged for the touch of a man's fingers.

If he wasn't mistaken, the smell of chocolate-chip cookies was wafting out the open door. As if the sight of her wasn't enough to make him feel weak with longing!

He had never felt so happy to see someone in his whole life, as if a box inside him he had deliberately closed was bursting open. And it contained the sun. His whole life seemed to go from dark to light. The part of him that he had tried to keep cold, for his own protection and for hers, was melting faster than spring ice off Glover's Pond.

How was he going to keep her from seeing that?

He slipped inside his apartment, and she turned and glanced at him.

She was wearing makeup. Just a hint of it that made her cheekbones look high, her mouth sensual, her eyes astounding.

Was it seeing her here, in his space, instead of against the familiar backdrop of Sugar Maple Grove, that made him see her so clearly?

Or was it the fact she had become, completely, that woman he had glimpsed striding away from him the night he had last seen her? Sophie looked as if she had come into herself totally, was completely comfortable with her power.

Her smile rose up to meet the sun, and the brilliance of it meeting that lid-off-the-sun feeling inside him created a sensation akin to that of trying to ride fireworks.

"What the hell?" He kept his voice gruff, he folded his arms over his chest.

"Hello, Brand. Nice to see you, too."

He frowned at her. "How did you get in here?"

"Your dad told me you probably kept the key above the door."

"My dad knows you're here?"

"He thinks I'm the best thing that could ever happen to you."

That's not the point. Of course she's the best thing that could ever happen to me. The point is, I'm not the best thing that could ever happen to her. Hadn't she read the letters? Didn't she get it?

"This is California, not Sugar Maple Grove," he said, skirting the issue of best things. "You can't just be in here baking up cookies with the doors unlocked."

She held up a hand. "Stop. No more. If I need protection, I'll buy a rottweiler."

"You don't need protection in Sugar Maple Grove. Which is where you belong."

"Not up to *you* to decide where *I* belong."

Well, he'd been right about her coming into her power. "Have you been messing with my kitchen?"

"If I'm going to be staying for a while, I thought I might as well put a few things away. Buy you a cookie sheet. What's a kitchen without a cookie sheet?"

"It's called a bachelor pad. And what do you mean, if you're going to be staying? Here? In my house, *here?* No, you're not."

"Yes, I am. Until you come to your senses."

"Sophie, there is nothing sensible about you coming across the country to be here, and then thinking you are staying here."

"Oh," she said, "luckily, I'm not the one who has to come to my senses. And I'm all done being sensible. I figured out playing it safe is the most dangerous thing I could do. Stagnating. That's a dangerous thing."

Brand could tell she had not been stagnating. It was in everything about her: the confident curl of her lips, the sashay of her hips, the light in her eyes that was both playful and unsettlingly powerful.

"You're not staying here," he said, curtly.

"You look exhausted," Sophie said soothingly. "Come have some cookies, right out of the oven. Your mom's recipe."

He knew the smart thing to do would be to back out that door and hightail it for safe ground. But he was in the grip of something larger than himself, and he could not break its hold.

Brand moved into his apartment, reluctantly sat at the kitchen table. He could smell her.

Clean and tangy, pure and promising. Promising a respite from what he had just come from.

"Have a cookie," she coaxed.

He knew he shouldn't touch those cookies, but the battle was short. He took one, took a bite, closed his eyes in pleasure.

"Do you want milk?"

"I don't have milk," he said crankily, opening his eyes, staring at her, thinking, *This is a dream, and I'm going to wake up alone. When did I start hating being alone so much?*

Chase her away. Let her have the truth. Make her go back out that door. "It goes sour when I have to leave. That's what I do. I leave. For long periods of time. I can't always say when I'm coming back."

He hesitated. "I can't always say *if* I'm coming back."

He found a glass of milk in front of him. *Don't drink it,* he ordered himself. It was probably like some secret nectar. Once he drank it, he'd be lost.

He took a sip.

And was lost. He'd been living on his own for eight years. And this was the first time he had ever felt as if he'd come home.

The cookies, the milk, Sophie watching him, the exhaustion, the people he couldn't save.

He put his head in his hands and drew a deep and shuddering breath.

And felt her hand on his shoulder.

"It's okay," she said softly. "I have your back."

"You don't even know what that means," he snapped. "I just took fourteen people out of a hotel where they'd been taken hostage. Only twelve of them were alive."

She was behind him. Her arms curled around his neck, and he found his head pillowed in unbelievable softness.

"Aww, Brand," she whispered.

And that was all. How could it possibly be enough?

How could that possibly lighten the weight he carried inside of him?

He was aware that this feeling could become addictive. Before he knew it, he wasn't going to be able to let her go, even if he wanted to.

"I could have died," he said. "What kind of life is that to offer someone? It isn't. You're going to have to leave."

"No."

"Yes."

"No." Every bit as strong as his *yes,* possibly stronger.

"You can't stay here without me inviting you."

"Kick me out, then."

But he couldn't. Already there was something about her being here that he wanted to sink into and hang on to. Forever.

The one word he could not have in his vocabulary!

He grabbed at a straw. "It won't be good for your reputation in Sugar Maple Grove if you stay here with me," he warned her.

She actually laughed at that. "I'm not worried about my reputation."

"I am," he sputtered. "You can't stay here. It's not decent."

"I'm staying. I'll leave it up to you how decent or indecent it becomes. For a while, anyway."

"I don't think your grandmother would approve of this."

"That just shows you don't know the first thing about my grandmother. You should know more, since she was letting her secret self out when she spoke German around you."

"My dad's going to kill me if I let you stay here." The straws he was reaching for were becoming weaker and weaker and they both knew it.

"No. He encouraged me to come. He said that time was too short."

"Oh, hell, the time-is-short lecture."

"It's true, Brand. Let's not waste any more of it. You just told me you could have died on the mission you were on. Do you know how I would have felt if that had happened? I would have felt as if I had wasted the most important moments of my life. Moments that I should have been with you and weren't. Brand, I—"

He knew what she was going to say. He knew it. "Don't. Don't say it." It would be worse than the cookies and the milk. It would swamp him. It would make him weak when he wanted to be strong.

But she wasn't a woman who was going to rein herself in. She said it anyway.

"I'm here because I love you. I don't want to waste another minute."

What could a guy say to that? He could say he loved her back, but that seemed as if it was giving in without even making an effort to keep her safe from loving him.

"I'm here to court you, Brand Sheridan."

"This won't end the way you want it to," he said miserably.

"Ah," she said, not the least perturbed or concerned. "I don't think either of us can know that until the courtship is over."

I love you.

He was right. Her words swamped him, stole his resolve to be strong, stole his sense of knowing right from wrong.

"What about your job?" he asked, a last desperate reach for a straw. "You can't leave your job. You can't burn your bridges for something that isn't going to work."

"Oh, I brought all my research with me. The Historical

Society's board of directors all thought it was a wonderful idea for me to get away for a while to put together the draft of the book on Sugar Maple Grove during the Second World War. I can work on it while you're on a mission."

"I only have one bedroom," he pointed out.

"It's okay. I'll sleep on the couch."

"The hell you will. I'll sleep on the couch."

She smiled at him. "If you insist."

And somehow he realized he had been *tricked* into agreeing she would stay here. But that didn't mean she'd win. She could stay here if she wanted. He could ignore her.

Except he couldn't. Because that night, after he'd gorged himself on cookies that already had some kind of love nectar baked into them, she talked him into a game of Scrabble and trounced him with thorough enjoyment. And after Scrabble, she went into his bedroom and came out in a little pair of pure-white baby-doll pajamas that made his mouth go dry and his heart beat in double time.

"We need a few rules around the courtship," he said. "Don't expect a kiss good-night. These quarters are too close. There's no telling where that could lead."

Especially with her in baby dolls!

She'd looked at him with wide-eyed innocence, and said, "You're absolutely right. I should have thought of that myself." And then she'd blown him a kiss, and gone into the bedroom and shut the door behind her.

Naturally, he wasn't safe, and she'd known it! When he went to use his bathroom, a red bra was hanging over his shower rod. Sophie in a red bra. No, not just any red bra, that one. That one that looked as if it was constructed from raw silk threads and fog.

Less true words than *I'll sleep on the couch* had never been spoken. It was soon evident to him his days of sleeping were over.

Because he had milk he could have cereal for breakfast. He tried to read the box and not notice her sitting across from him in her baby dolls, reading the paper that was his, sipping her coffee, her naked legs folded under her. No candy-floss pink on the nails anymore.

Fire-engine red. To match her bra.

"Look, we need a few more rules," he said hoarsely, "For the courtship."

"I'm listening."

"No red bra in the bathroom. And you can't wear those around the house."

She pretended she was thinking about it. "How about a trade?"

"A trade?" he asked warily.

"I don't leave my underwear around. You take me bike-riding after work. Along the boardwalk. Maybe we can stop and have hot dogs for supper."

He considered. "Okay."

And that's how the courtship of Brand Sheridan started: with bike rides and hot dogs. Then, in exchange for the removal of the black bra from his shower rod, she wanted to try in-line skating. By the time she wanted to go to a live theater presentation he knew it was no use bargaining over where she left her skimpy, sexy little undergarments.

Having her underwear out of the bathroom wasn't helping him sleep at night. The moratorium on the baby dolls was a farce. Her pink pajamas, with long sleeves, full legs and the cartoon monkeys doing yoga on them were as sexy as the baby dolls, though logically he knew that wasn't possible.

She liked having cocoa before bed, and they would stay up way too late talking, laughing, sometimes playing Scrabble.

He was now so sleep-deprived, he was getting in trouble at work. He was making stupid, novice mistakes. His concentration was shot. He was late for roll call because he phoned her at lunchtime to make sure she had locked the damn door. He didn't respond to a direct command because he was mulling over the fact she had *laughed* when he told her to lock the door, to go make sure it was locked.

"Is your job always so exhausting?" she asked him soothingly when he dragged himself in that night. "This will help. I made you a treat." It was roast beef. And Yorkshire pudding. He already knew. His mother's recipe.

"This isn't a courtship," he told her, three days in. "It's a hijacking. It's a hostage-taking. I hope you get tired of this soon!"

Before he fell in any more deeply.

But she didn't and he did.

There was something about not being in Sugar Maple Grove that set them free. The familiar backdrop was gone. Nobody was watching. She wasn't the girl next door; he wasn't the boy next door.

They were getting to know each other on a different level—as adults, as equals. She wasn't his sweet pea anymore.

She was a woman. Fascinating. Multifaceted. Sensual. Fun. Smart. Curious. She had an unexpected taste for adventure.

At her insistence, they found a climbing wall, and she showed him what she had learned.

Brand had been climbing all his adult life, but it had never been quite the experience it was going up the wall behind her, her harness doing things to her butt that made it more sexy than the baby dolls!

Sophie loved trying new things, was so *ready* to leap out of the comfort zone of a small-town girl with limited experiences available to her.

She thought it was fun to take public transit! She couldn't get enough of the ocean and bought her own snorkel and fins. She planned picnics on the beach so they could watch the whales go by and the sun sink down.

And he, reluctantly at first and then with more and more enthusiasm, loved finding new things for her to try.

She especially liked ethnic food. He even found a Middle Eastern restaurant that had rose-petal ice cream.

And for all that she embraced everything new, she was still the old Sophie, too, a woman content to work on her collection of stories for the Historical Society, and to try out cookie recipes on him.

As he grew more exhausted by her courtship, lying awake on that couch at night imagining her sleeping in his bed, imagining what it would be like to give in totally, go to her, taste her, hold her, have her, she grew more invigorated.

The exhaustion was taking a toll. His walls were coming down. He was telling her things she had no business knowing. They just slipped out of him in these intimate little moments she had a way of creating.

Who knew intimacy could have so little to do with red underwear?

He told her things he couldn't expect her to handle. He told her about burying his best friend three days after they'd been deployed overseas. He told her about playing the role of Brian Sinclair and betraying every single person who had come to like and trust him.

He told her about the hotel rescue and the face of a

blonde woman he hadn't been able to save who haunted his dreams.

But the thing was, she was handling his secrets just fine. And every day that he trusted her with a little more of himself, something eased in him.

Something that had been held way too tight for way too long began to relax.

She'd been there two weeks when he got it. It wasn't a flash of light. He was just worn right out.

"You win," he told her, when he came in after an extra-hard day of trying to train in his sleep-deprived state. She'd made strawberry lemonade. "You win, Sophie. I surrender."

He hoped she knew that words more foreign to a warrior had never been spoken.

Nor had they ever been spoken with such heartfelt relief.

"No," he said, staring at her, feeling the blessed relief of surrendering, allowing himself to contemplate for the first time exactly what *that* meant. "Wait. You don't win. I win. Because even though I don't deserve you, and even though I don't want to inflict this lifestyle on you, you're still here. And I have a feeling you're just not going to go away."

"You're right, I'm not."

He went to her. He allowed himself to touch her. She was so soft. Her skin was so beautiful and so flawless. His fingers felt as if they had waited all his life for this moment of absolute surrender when they could worship her with their tips.

He took the plump temptation of her lips in his and allowed himself to feel it and not fight it.

Her lips opening to his, inviting him deeper, calling him to know all of her—that was exciting! Every single thing that had ever passed itself off as excitement before that had been a lie.

"I love you," he whispered. "I want to marry you. I feel as if I will die if I don't have you to come home to, you to look forward to for the rest of my life. I feel as if I was dying of loneliness and didn't even know until you came, Sophie. You didn't court me. You rescued me."

There was something bigger than both of them in the air when her eyes met his, and she teased his lips with her tongue, and slipped her hand inside his shirt.

He had a sense of the adventure that had been his life not ending, but beginning in a brand-new way.

A way that required more of him than had ever been required before.

All of life would be a courtship, a dance, a celebration.

"Sophie, will you marry me?"

One word. His whole heart stood still, his whole life stood in the balance while he waited to hear that one word.

And when he heard it, it was as if her soul had spoken to him. It was not so much a word as an affirmation of the power of love to win.

To bring a lost warrior home. And to heal him once he got there.

"Yes."

EPILOGUE

THE Internet was an amazing thing, Brand thought, but even he was sometimes newly amazed by it.

For instance, if you typed in the phrase *What Makes a Small Town Tick,* imagine that you could be transported back over time to a grainy video of a small-town girl about to win a big-time speech competition.

Funny, she wasn't as geeky as he remembered her being at twelve, right around the age she'd been when she had first moved in next door to him.

She was cute as a button, tiny on that big stage, brave somehow.

Her voice had a little quaver to it as she started talking about all the charms of small-town living, but it grew stronger as she warmed up. She talked about funny things like the time the rumor had gone through town like wildfire that the President was coming to Sugar Maple Grove. She talked about picnics and Blue Rock and ice cream on hot nights. She talked about front porches and unlocked doors.

And then she talked about a little boy who had gotten cancer and how the whole town circled that family and raised money for him. She talked about the Francis house burning to the ground and the old-fashioned barn-building that had raised it back up.

Finally, she looked directly into a camera she probably had not known was there, and she said in a voice that wasn't quivering at all anymore, in a voice that was strong and soft with conviction, "What makes a small town tick? Love does."

He froze it right there, on a little carrot-topped girl with braces and freckles. He could see in that ancient video a hint of the woman she was going to be. He could see the beginning of the bravery that had gotten her through some terrible things.

He could see the beginning of a woman brave enough to come after him. Brave enough to know he *needed* her to love him, he *needed* to love her.

All those years ago, when she had said it was love that made a small town tick, she had missed a bigger truth.

Love was what made her tick.

Watching Sophie's younger self, he allowed himself to think, if it's a little girl will she look like that? Be like that?

They had been married three years. He had left FREES and returned to what he had always liked most about his work. Brand and Sophie had started a school here in the shadow of the Green Mountains, thirty miles from where he was born.

The school, called Higher Ground, was for vertical-rescue specialists, and his reputation was now cemented.

He did what he loved every single day, working the ropes, teaching others: lowering, highlines, Stokes baskets, technical, rappelling. Sophie ran the office, using all those considerable organizational skills she'd used at the Historical Society and putting together her book.

They worked together, they lived together, the love just seemed to grow deeper and better every day. Love. That was the real higher ground.

It was as perfect a life as any man could ask for.

"Brand, what are you doing?"

Her voice was so soft behind him. She came and leaned on his shoulder, he felt the gentle brush of a taut belly, the little life inside there kicked at him.

"I couldn't sleep."

She looked over his shoulder at the computer screen and laughed. "Good grief, Brand, this is not what most men are looking at on the Internet in the middle of the night when they can't sleep."

"What do you know about most men, Mrs. Sheridan?"

"That they aren't anything like you." She wrapped her arms around his neck, played with the diamond stud in his ear.

The hole where it had been pierced refused to grow over. She had gotten him the diamond stud instead of a wedding band, knowing he didn't want to wear a band that could get caught when he worked with ropes.

He didn't consider himself an earring kind of guy, but she thought it was sexy as hell, and he loved it when she got *that* look on her face just from looking at it.

Once, his younger self had chased excitement and danger, had been fooled by those false highs. Brand had a growing sense of having *needed* to be that younger man, he felt as tolerant of his younger self as he did of hers.

He had needed to be who he was to be able to recognize truth when it found him.

There was nothing more exciting than this. Loving another human being. Creating another human being.

Now he was a man who knew it didn't get much better than Sophie's delicate fingers toying with the diamond stud in his ear as she looked over his shoulder at the computer screen.

Considering how big her belly was, it was probably

some kind of sin how her fingers on his ear were making him feel.

"I was kind of cute back then," she decided.

"You still are kind of cute."

"I know."

They both laughed. He loved the confidence in her, the radiant beauty, the sassiness of a woman who was loved above all things and knew it.

"I was a nerd," she decided. "But a cute nerd."

"She's going to be just like you," he decided. "It's a good thing she'll have me. She'll need me to protect her."

"We don't even know if it's a girl."

"I do," he said stubbornly. "I know it's a girl. I've kind of missed having someone who needs me. I was born for it."

"To protect?"

"To be a daddy."

"Yes," Sophie whispered, "you were. And Brand? The daddy thing?"

"Uh-huh?"

"It's going to be sooner rather than later, because I'm having this funny little pain. Right here."

She guided his hand to her belly.

Brand was a man who had looked into the face of death and never flinched from it. He was a man who made his living scrambling up and down incredible, stomach-dropping heights. He was a man who, for his entire life, had pushed himself to heroism, who had welcomed risk and made friends with danger.

He swallowed hard. She was the one person who knew he was only a man, after all. She was the one person in all the world around whom he could let down his guard.

But not tonight. Tonight he would be as strong as a man could ever hope to be. Because she was going to have to be as strong as a woman could ever hope to be. He could match that. He had to.

This was what he'd been born to do.

"Don't you worry, Sophie Sheridan," he said. "I've got your back."

Sophie laughed. "You're terrified."

She was the one person in the world who could see right through him.

"Your dad and my grandma are on their way," she told him gently. "Just in case I get a little too preoccupied to have *your* back."

Once, in the arrogance and restlessness of youth, Brand Sheridan had walked away from all a family meant and all that it offered. He had thought he needed other things more: excitement, thrills, adventures.

But it was the nature of love how thoroughly it forgave a man who realized his errors, who came to know there was only one *real* adventure.

Brand got to his feet and took Sophie's hand. He looked at her long and hard and deep.

And the word that came to his lips and his mind and his heart was not a battle cry at all, but an affirmation.

"Honor," he said softly, his voice strong and sure.

And then he scooped up his wife as if she weighed nothing at all, and with her arms around her neck and her sweet breath stirring against his chest, Brand Sheridan moved effortlessly, fearlessly, toward the future.

Coming Next Month

Available August 10, 2010

LARGER-PRINT BOOKS!

GET 2 FREE LARGER-PRINT NOVELS PLUS
2 FREE GIFTS!

HARLEQUIN® *Romance*®

From the Heart, For the Heart

HRLP10R2

HARLEQUIN®

A *Romance*

FOR EVERY MOOD™

Spotlight on

Heart & Home

Heartwarming romances
where love can happen
right when you least expect it.

See the next page to enjoy a sneak peek
from Harlequin® American Romance®,
a Heart and Home series.

CATHHHAR10

Five hunky Texas single fathers—five stories from Cathy Gillen Thacker's LONE STAR DADS *miniseries. Here's an excerpt from the latest, THE MOMMY PROPOSAL from Harlequin American Romance.*

"I hear you work miracles," Nate Hutchinson drawled. Brooke Mitchell had just stepped into his lavishly appointed office in downtown Fort Worth, Texas.

"Sometimes, I do." Brooke smiled and took the sexy financier's hand in hers, shook it briefly.

"Good." Nate looked her straight in the eye. "Because I'm in need of a home makeover—fast. The son of an old friend is coming to live with me."

She was still tingling from the feel of his warm palm. "Temporarily or permanently?"

"If all goes according to plan, I'll adopt Landry by summer's end."

Brooke had heard the founder of Nate Hutchinson Financial Services was eligible, wealthy and generous to a fault. She hadn't known he was in the market for a family, but she supposed she shouldn't be surprised. But Brooke had figured a man as successful and handsome as Nate would want one the old-fashioned way. *Not that this was any of her business...*

"So what's the child like?" she asked crisply, trying not to think how the marine-blue of Nate's dress shirt deepened the hue of his eyes.

"I don't know." Nate took a seat behind his massive antique mahogany desk. He relaxed against the smooth leather of the chair. "I've never met him."

"Yet you've invited this kid to live with you permanently?"

"It's complicated. But I'm sure it's going to be fine."

Obviously Nate Hutchinson knew as little about teenage

boys as he did about decorating. But that wasn't her problem. Finding a way to do the assignment without getting the least bit emotionally involved was.

Find out how a young boy brings Nate and Brooke together in THE MOMMY PROPOSAL, coming August 2010 from Harlequin American Romance.

HAREXP0810

Love Inspired.
HISTORICAL
INSPIRATIONAL HISTORICAL ROMANCE

Bestselling author

JILLIAN HART

brings readers
a new heartwarming story in

Patchwork Bride

Meredith Worthington is returning to
Angel Falls, Montana, to follow her dream
of becoming a teacher. And perhaps get to know
Shane Connelly, the intriguing new wrangler on
her father's ranch. Shane can't resist her charm
even though she reminds him of everything he'd like
to forget. But will love have time to blossom before
she discovers the secret he's been hiding all along?

*Available in August
wherever books are sold.*

www.SteepleHill.com

Steeple
Hill®
LIH82841

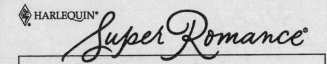